高职高专
英语泛读教程

主编：龚 耀

编者：张秀芹 姚友本 易 华 伏艳
何正英 李 华 刘欣娟

外语教学与研究出版社
FOREIGN LANGUAGE TEACHING AND RESEARCH PRESS
北京 BEIJING

图书在版编目(CIP)数据

高职高专英语泛读教程. 2 / 龚耀主编；张秀芹等编 .— 北京：外语教学与研究出版社，2009.3

ISBN 978－7－5600－8218－9

Ⅰ. 高… Ⅱ. ①龚… ②张… Ⅲ. 英语—阅读教学—高等学校：技术学校—教材 Ⅳ. H319.4

中国版本图书馆 CIP 数据核字 (2009) 第 033471 号

出 版 人：于春迟
责任编辑：姚雪燕
封面设计：赵　欣
版式设计：张苏梅
出版发行：外语教学与研究出版社
社　　址：北京市西三环北路 19 号 (100089)
网　　址：http://www.fltrp.com
印　　刷：北京新华印刷厂
开　　本：787×1092　1/16
印　　张：9.75
版　　次：2009 年 3 月第 1 版　2009 年 3 月第 1 次印刷
书　　号：ISBN 978－7－5600－8218－9
定　　价：15.90 元

*　　*　　*

编写说明

　　《高职高专英语泛读教程》以当前我国高职高专英语教学的实际需要为出发点，以培养学生的英语综合应用能力为目标，以突出和强化学生阅读技能训练与培养为目的，而设计、开发的一套贴近高职学生生活，实用新颖，学、考并重的全新阅读教材。

　　本教材依据《高职高专教育英语课程教学基本要求》，结合高等学校英语应用能力A、B级考试和大学英语四级考试，按照实用、够用的原则，设计、编排各单元的内容和体例，旨在帮助学生培养良好的阅读习惯，掌握实用的英语阅读知识和技巧，提高英语的文字处理能力，顺利通过A、B级和四级考试，并为学生的可持续性发展创造良好条件。

　　《高职高专英语泛读教程》共三册，每册十个单元。每单元的编排体例如下：

　　一、Passage A：每单元围绕一个主题，广泛选取近年来各种题材的既有知识性、思想性，又有较强可读性的精美原文作为主阅读课文。这些课文语言规范、地道，难度恰到好处。难点、重点、背景知识都作了相应的介绍和注释，并针对阅读课文设置了紧密结合A、B级和四级考试题型的多项练习，包括选择填空、常用词汇操练（第一册B级、第二册A级、第三册四级）、回答问题等，以检查学生阅读理解的能力。

　　二、Reading Skills：全面、系统又深入浅出地介绍了高职高专学生需要掌握的一些实用英语阅读技巧。文字介绍简单、易懂，所配例题清楚、明了，设置的练习针对性强，能有效帮助学生尽快提高阅读水平。

　　三、Passage B：文章和单元主题相关，主要用来训练学生的快速阅读能力。其难度和主阅读课文的难度相当或略低。生词量控制在B级（第一册）、A级（第二册）、四级（第三册）考试要求之内。对较难的生词和短语，都标注了中文意思。练习旨在检查学生对文章细节、主旨大意的理解和运用阅读技巧的熟练程度。

　　四、Reading Comprehension from PRETCO：从历年真题（第一册B级，第二册A级）中，精选两篇和单元主题相关的阅读理解文章，对学生进行更深层次、更加实用的训练和测试，充分体现学、考并重，把语言知识、技能的传授和实际考试训练有机结合在一起。

五、Reading for Fun: 挑选轻松、幽默、健康的有趣短文，让学生体验阅读的乐趣，在会心一笑之中，放松紧张的身心，消除阅读的疲劳，提高兴趣，拓宽知识面。

本书是《高职高专英语泛读教程》第二册，由龚耀主编（编写第六、七、十单元）。编委有：张秀芹（第一单元）、姚友本（第二单元）、易华（第三单元）、伏艳（第四单元）、何正英（第五单元）、李华（第八单元）、刘欣娟（第九单元）。

在本书的编写过程中，我们参阅了大量的国内外资料和文章，得到了外语教学与研究出版社的大力支持和帮助。由于我们编写时间紧，水平有限，书中难免有不妥之处。恳请使用本书的同行批评指正。

编者

2009年1月

Contents

Unit 1
Advertisements Everywhere

Passage A   Advertising—True or False?

The amount of advertising and marketing has exploded over the past decade; studies acknowledge that on average we see 3,000 ads per day. At the gas pumps, in the movie theatre, on the buses, during sporting events—advertising is impossible to avoid. Even outer space isn't safe from commercialization: the Russian space program launched a rocket bearing a 30-foot Pizza Hut logo, and some companies have investigated placing ads in space that will be visible from the earth. The challenge of the future may be finding public and private space that are free of advertising. Advertising is a good way to promote new products, but on the other hand, false or deceptive advertisements can have negative influence on people. Let's look at the following two advertisements:

This really makes me want to buy chicken...

Workers shown on TV singing with their mouths full have prompted a flood of complaints from Britons concerned over the depiction of bad manners. The commercial for Kentucky Fried Chicken became Britain's most complained about ad, with 1,671 members of the public contacting the Advertising Standards Authority (ASA). Offended viewers said it encouraged bad manners in children by making it appear funny to sing or speak while eating and 41 of those who complained said their children had aped the ad. But the ASA rejected all complaints and dismissed fears of an epidemic of children eating open-mouthedly. "As teaching good table manners is an ongoing process needing frequent reminders at meal times, we do not agree that the advertisement would have a harmful effect," the authority said in its ruling. Nearly all those who complained said they found it unpleasant to watch. The ad used subtitles to explain what the three call center staff were singing as they munched KFC salads, leading some viewers to complain that it mocked people with speech and hearing barriers. It ended with one of the women answering a phone singing "hello, emergency helpline" which prompted others to complain that it implied call center staff were unprofessional. KFC said it intended

the commercial to be light-hearted. The previous record for complaints over a television commercial was the 860 complaints filed against a Wrigley's gum commercial that showed a man regurgitating a dog. The commercial shows a man waking up on a sofa after a heavy night out. Then he vomits and a paw emerges from his mouth—followed by a scruffy grey dog. The man eats some chewing gum which makes the dog disappear. A caption appears stating "Avoid dog breath". Parents complained that the scene frightened their children and made them feel sick. Ad watchdogs agreed with the complaints.

Size matters in ban on sandwich ad

A television commercial for KFC was banned by Britain's advertising watchdog because it said the fast food chain misled customers into thinking its mini chicken sandwiches were larger than they really are. The Advertising Standards Authority said that after it bought three mini chicken fillet sandwiches from a London KFC it agreed with five complaints about the ad—which included a close-up of a sandwich in a woman's hands. "We believed the visuals were likely to mislead viewers over the actual size," the agency said, "We noted that the bun shown in the advertisement was significantly thicker than the burgers we purchased; that there was more filling and the lettuce was a different type." The ASA ordered that the ad, created by London-based agency Bartle Bogle Hegarty (BBH), not be shown again in its existing form. KFC argued that the woman in the ad simply may have small hands, although it said the actress was not cast for that reason. The chain also said the burger's name and price—99 pence ($1.86)—implied that it was smaller than a normal fillet burger. The ASA said it did not think that was sufficient to alert consumers that the sandwich was smaller than it appeared.

Both the two advertisements show some negative effects. Actually every coin has two sides. Advertising is no exception. People should become wiser and learn to use their brains when facing a beautiful and attractive advertisement.

New Words

1. acknowlegde	v.	认为，公认
2. alert	v.	警告，使警觉
3. ape	v.	模仿
4. ban	n.	禁令
5. barrier	n.	障碍
6. bun	n.	小圆面包
7. burger	n.	汉堡
8. cast	v.	分配角色，指定演员
9. commercialization	n.	商业化，商品化
10. deceptive	a.	骗人的，欺骗性的
11. depiction	n.	描写叙述

12. epidemic	*n.*	（坏事的）发生次数陡增，频率突增
13. fillet	*n.*	肉片
14. lettuce	*n.*	生菜
15. mini	*a.*	迷你的，小的
16. mock	*v.*	嘲笑，嘲弄
17. munch	*v.*	用力嚼，大声嚼
18. private	*a.*	私人的
19. prompt	*v.*	激起，唤起
20. regurgitate	*v.*	吐出
21. subtitle	*n.*	字幕
22. visible	*a.*	看得见的
23. visual	*n.*	画面，图像
24. vomit	*v.*	吐出，呕吐
25. watchdog	*n.*	监督者（个人或集体）

Notes

1. …the Russian space program launched a rocket bearing a 30-foot Pizza Hut logo…
……俄罗斯的太空计划发射了一枚载有一个30英寸的必胜客比萨商标的火箭……
launch a rocket: 发射一枚火箭。类似地，发射一颗卫星可译为launch a satellite
bear a logo: 带有一个商标。 bear在文中的意思是"标有，有明显标记"。
Pizza Hut: 从1958年美国年轻的卡尼兄弟以一间只有25个座位、像小屋（hut）一样的比萨餐厅开始创业至今，短短51年，必胜客已发展成为全球最大的比萨饼专卖连锁企业。

2. The commercial for Kentucky Fried Chicken became Britain's most complained about ad, with 1,671 members of the public contacting the Advertising Standards Authority (ASA).
这则肯德基的电视广告成了英国投诉量最多的广告，有1,671名民众为此向英国广告审查局（ASA）表示不满。
Advertising Standards Authority (ASA): 英国广告审查局
complain about sth.: 抱怨，表达不满或愤怒的感受，例如，She is always complaining about something.
Kentucky Fried Chicken: 肯德基（KFC）源于美国，创建于1930年，是世界著名的炸鸡快餐连锁企业。

3. The ASA ordered that the ad, created by London-based agency Bartle Bogle Hegarty (BBH), not be shown again in its existing form.
ASA已经下令，电视台不得再原样播出这则由伦敦广告公司BBH制作的广告。
London-based agency: 总部在伦敦的公司，机构

Bartle Bogle Hegarty: BBH是闻名世界，以创意著称的广告公司，在新加坡，东京，纽约，上海等城市设有分公司。

in the existing form: 原样

Exercises

1. Choose the best answer.

1) Why did the Russian space program launch a rocket bearing a 30-foot Pizza Hut logo?

   A. To show their technology of exploring outer space.

   B. To show a commercial advertisement.

   C. To send food to the astronauts.

   D. To make the rocket more beautiful.

2) What was people's attitude towards the commercial for Kentucky Fried Chicken (Paragraph 2)?

   A. Doubtful.

   B. Critical.

   C. Positive.

   D. Indifferent.

3) What was the ASA's reaction to people's complaints about the commercial for Kentucky Fried Chicken (Paragraph 2)?

   A. The ASA supported their complaints.

   B. The ASA turned a deaf ear to their complaints.

   C. The ASA rejected their complaints.

   D. It is not mentioned in the text.

4) How did KFC respond to people's complaints about its commercial (Paragraph 2)?

   A. It apologized to the audience.

   B. It explained that it intended the commercial to be light-hearted.

   C. It cancelled the commercial.

   D. It redesigned the commercial.

5) What does the passage mainly tell us?

   A. Advertisements are deceptive.

   B. We shouldn't believe advertisements.

   C. Advertisements bring convenience to our lives.

   D. The misleading or deceptive advertisements may produce negative social effects.

2. Complete the statements that follow the questions.

1) What is the function of advertising?

Advertising is a good way to _____.

2) Which organization is in charge of overseeing advertisements in Britain?

_____.

3) Why did so many people complain about the commercial for Kentucky Fried Chicken?

Because they thought it encouraged bad manners in children, some of whom had actually

_____.

4) Why did the ASA ban the KFC sandwich ad (Paragraph 3)?

Because it _____ its mini chicken fillet sandwiches were larger than

they really are.

5) How did KFC argue for its banned sandwich ad (Paragraph 3)?

KFC argued that the woman in the ad simply may have small hands, although it said the

actress was _____ that reason.

3. Match the following words with the definitions below and then fill in the blanks with their proper forms.

investigate	deceptive	prompt	epidemic	barrier
vomit	ban	visual	significantly	sufficient
alert	commercial	emerge	standard	acknowledge

1) (*noun*) sth. that prevents or hinders the progress or movement

Wang is an English major. He has no language _____ in communicating with

English-speaking people.

2) (*noun*) an advertisement on television or radio

Nowadays there are so many _____ in our society that we wonder whether they

can be trusted or not.

3) (*adjective*) tending to cheat

Don't believe it! It is a _____ advertisement.

4) (*adverb*) importantly or meaningfully

To our pride, the *Shenzhou* VII mission has been _____ successful.

5) (*verb*) to bring food or drink up from your stomach out through your mouth

He _____ all he had eaten.

6) (*noun*) a sudden increase in the amount of times that sth. bad happens

There has recently been a(n) _____ of car thefts in the city.

7) (*verb*) to give rise to; inspire

The campus accident _____ a review of school safety rules and regulations.

8) (*verb*) to observe or inquire into sth. in detail

The policeman concentrated all his attention on _____ the robbery to the exclusion of his leisure and entertainment.

9) (*verb*) to prohibit, especially by official order

The movie _____ in Arabian world because it has offended the Arabian people.

10) (*adjective*) as much as is needed for a particular purpose; enough

His income is _____ to keep him comfortable.

11) (*noun*) a picture, chart, or other presentation that appeals to the sense of sight, used in promotion or for illustration

Many commercials on TV, though always boasting, have striking _____.

12) (*verb*) to admit the existence, reality, or truth of sth.

He _____ that the purchase of the second-hand car had been a mistake.

13) (*verb*) to appear or come out from somewhere

The sun _____ from behind the clouds.

14) (*verb*) to notify sb. of approaching danger or action; warn

The flashing red light _____ motorists to trouble ahead.

15) (*noun*) an acknowledged measure of comparison for quantitative or qualitative value; a criterion

There is no absolute _____ for beauty.

Reading Skills

Ⓓistinguishing Between Facts and Opinions

区分事实与观点

　　区分事实与观点的能力对于我们更深入地理解阅读材料有着非常重要的意义。作者在写作过程中，往往在介绍一个事实（fact）的同时，会阐明自己的观点（opinion），表达对事实的看法和认识。

　　观点是指个人的信仰、判断或感情等，是个人对事实的一种理解，与读者的观点相同或者相悖。表示观点的词或短语通常有believe, think, opinion, feel, suggest, appear, seem, could, perhaps, likely, probably, possible, convince等。同时还有一些感情色彩比较强烈的修饰词也表示作者的观点，如disgusting, good, great, nice, terrible, beautiful, ugly, pretty, the lowest, the best, the worst等。也有这样的情况，作者并不用以上这些词或短语，而是开门见山、直截了当地表达自己的想法和观点。我们在阅读时，要注意识别。

　　事实是支撑观点的内容，是广泛为人们所接受的、真实存在的东西，它能够被证据证明是正确的或是错误的。表示事实范畴的词或短语通常有research, studies, findings, show, find, discover, prove等。

Facts:

1) The rate of extinction has speeded up unnaturally over the last 400 years, rising sharply since 1900. This increase in the rate of extinction is directly related to the increase in the human population over the same period of time.

2) At major athletic events, it is not uncommon to find 90,000 or 100,000 people sitting in the stands. On the playing field are two dozen athletes, maybe fewer.

3) Today there are more than 55 million phone subscribers in Britain, a huge leap from less than 10 million users in 1997.

以上例句都是表示客观存在的事实。

Opinions:

4) Gratefulness is the key to a happy life that we hold in our hands, because if we are not grateful, then no matter how much we have we will not be happy—because we will always want to have something else or something more.

5) Success in marriage does not come merely through finding the right mate, but through being the right mate.

6) I would prefer even to fail with honor than to win by cheating.

以上例句都是作者所表达的观点、思想、看法、评论等。

Ⓔxercises

1. Read the following statements and decide whether they are facts (F) or opinions (O).

1) Wednesday is the longest day of the week.

2) Generally speaking, movies are more interesting than books.

3) Lucy is the prettiest girl in my class.

4) Cigarettes can't be advertised on TV in England.

5) Many school buildings are located in this district of the city.

6) The more I learn, the less I know.

7) The Shanghai Museum was first established in 1952, and in 1992 it acquired a new site in the downtown on People's Square.

8) He is among the best of our workers.

9) This book has a much larger circulation than that one.

10) Books are to mankind what memory is to the individual.

2. Read the following paragraph and answer the questions.

"Avoid the rush-hour" must be the slogan of large cities all over the world. Wherever you look, it's people, people, people. The trains which leave or arrive every few minutes are packed: an endless procession of human sardine (沙丁鱼) tins. The streets are so crowded, and there is hardly room to move on the pavements. The queues for buses reach staggering proportions (令人惊愕的比例). It takes ages for a bus to get to you because the traffic on the roads has virtually come to a standstill. So, living in a large modern city may not be as good as you think.

1) What is the author's opinion?

   _____.

2) What are the facts that support the opinion?
   a) _____.
   b) _____.
   c) _____.
   d) _____.

Passage B Television Advertising Leads to Unhealthy Habits in Children

Read the passage and judge whether the following statements are true (T) or false (F).

    1) Research shows that children under the age of eight tend to accept advertising messages as truthful, accurate and unbiased.

    2) ASA recommends that advertising targeting children under the age of eight should be restricted.

    3) It is estimated that advertisers spend more than $12 billion per year on advertising messages aimed at adults.

    4) The task force was appointed by the American government in 2000.

    5) According to the research, the average child watches more than 40,000 television commercials per year.

    6) The findings show that children can recall content from the ads to which they've been exposed.

    7) Advertisements primarily targeting adults have no influence on children.

    8) The research points out that advertisements of unhealthy food products encourage bad nutritional habits in children.

    9) To some extent, advertisements can cause parent-child conflicts when parents deny their children's requests for buying advertised products.

    10) APA recommends banning advertising primarily directed to young children of eight years and under.

Research shows that children under the age of eight are unable to critically comprehend televised advertising messages and are prone to (易于) accept advertising messages as truthful, accurate and unbiased. This can lead to unhealthy eating habits as evidenced by today's youth obesity epidemic. For these reasons, a task force of the American Psychological Association (APA) is recommending that advertising targeting children under the age of eight be restricted.

The task force, appointed by the APA in 2000, conducted an extensive review of the research literature in the area of advertising media, and its effects on children. It is estimated that advertisers spend more than $12 billion per year on advertising messages aimed at the youth market. Additionally, the average child watches more than 40,000 television commercials per year.

The six-member team of psychologists (心理学家) with expertise (专门知识) in child development, cognitive psychology and social psychology found that children under the age of eight lack the cognitive development to understand the persuasive intent of television advertising and are easily influenced by the advertising.

"While older children and adults understand the inherent bias (固有的偏见) of advertising, younger children do not, and therefore tend to interpret commercial claims and appeals as accurate and truthful information," said psychologist Dale Kunkel, PhD, Professor of Communication at the University of California at Santa Barbara and senior author of the task force's scientific report.

"Because younger children do not understand persuasive intent in advertising, they are easy targets for commercial persuasion," said psychologist Brian Wilcox, PhD, Professor of Psychology and Director of the Center on Children. "This is a critical concern because the most common products marketed to children are candies, sweets, sodas and snack foods. Such advertising of unhealthy food products to young children contributes to poor nutritional habits that may last a lifetime."

From a series of studies examining product choices, the findings show that children recall content from the ads to which they've been exposed and preference for a product has been shown to occur with as little as a single commercial exposure and strengthen with repeated exposures.

Furthermore, studies reviewed in the task force report show that these product preferences can affect children's product purchase requests, which can put pressure on parents' purchasing decisions and cause parent-child conflicts when parents deny their children's requests, said Kunkel and Wilcox.

Finally, in addition to the issues surrounding advertising directed to young children, said Kunkel, there are concerns regarding certain commercial campaigns primarily targeting adults that pose risks for child-viewers. "For example, beer ads are commonly shown during sports events and seen by millions of children, creating both brand familiarity and more positive attitudes toward drinking in children as young as 9—10 years of age. Another area of sensitive advertising content involves commercials for violent media products such as motion pictures and video games. Such ads contribute to a violent media culture which increases the likelihood of youngsters' aggressive behavior and desensitizes (使感觉迟钝，冷淡) children to real-world violence," said Dr. Kunkel.

According to the findings in the report, APA has developed the following recommendations:

1. Restrict advertising primarily directed to young children of eight years and under.

2. Ensure that disclosures (开诚布公的话) and disclaimers (不承担责任的声明) in advertising directed to children are conveyed in language clearly comprehensible to the intended audience. (e.g., use "You have to put it together" rather than "Some assembly required")

3. Investigate how young children comprehend and are influenced by advertising in new interactive media environments such as the Internet.

4. Examine the influence of advertising directed to children in the school and classroom.

Reading Comprehension from PRETCO

Task 1

Directions: *After reading the following passage, you will find 5 questions or unfinished statements. For each question or statement there are 4 choices marked A, B, C and D. You should make the correct choice and mark the corresponding letter with a single line through the center. (2003.06)*

Advertising informs consumers about new products available on the market. It gives us information about everything from shampoo to toothpaste to computers and cars. But the "information" it provides is actually very often "misinformation". It tells us the products' benefits but hides their disadvantages. Advertising not only leads us to buy things that we don't need and can't afford, but it also confuses our sense of reality.

Advertisements use many methods to get us buy their products. One of their most successful methods is to make us feel dissatisfied with ourselves and our imperfect lives. Advertisements show us who we aren't and what we don't have. Advertisements make us afraid that people won't like us if we don't use the advertised products.

If fear is the negative motive for buying a product, then wanting a good self-image is the positive reason for choosing it. Each of us has a mental picture of the kind of person we would like to be. Advertisers get psychologists to study the way consumers think and their reasons of choosing one brand instead of another. These experts tell advertisers about recent studies with colors and words. They have found that certain colors on the package of an attractive product will cause people to reach out and take that package instead of buying an identical product with different colors.

Many people believe that advertising does not affect them. They know that there is freedom to choose and they like to think they make wise choices. Unfortunately, they probably don't realize the powerful effect of advertising. They may not clearly understand that advertisers spend billions of dollars each year in aggressive competition for our money, and they are extremely successful.

1) What's the purpose of advertising?

    A. To introduce to people the features of their goods.

    B. To have people buy new products on the market.

    C. To make people know how to use their products.

    D. To tell people how to save money while buying things.

2) One of the disadvantages of advertising is to _____.

    A. lead people to buy bad-quality things

    B. make people confused about choosing goods

    C. make people buy more things than they need

    D. inform people about the products' benefits

3) Advertisements may make people think that _____,

    A. their lives are not good enough

    B. their behaviors are imperfect

    C. they don't have enough money to buy things

    D. they look poor without buying advertised things

4) What can psychologists tell the advertisers?

    A. The reasons for bad sale of some goods.

    B. Which brand is better than others.

    C. How to control the quality of goods.

    D. People's recent opinions about colors.

5) It is implied in the last paragraph that those who don't believe advertising _____.

    A. should refuse to buy goods advertised

    B. may also be influenced by advertising

    C. have more freedom to buy things than others

    D. can save money without buying the advertised goods

Task 2

Directions: *The following is an advertisement. After reading it, you are required to complete the outline below it. You should write your answers briefly (in no more than 3 words) in the blanks correspondingly. (2006. 06)*

The meeting is over. You're tired. Now will you get on a plane and rush back home to more work? Here is a better idea. Take a little time for yourself and relax at Holiday Inn.

All our 1,642 hotels worldwide have the best leisure facilities available. And the best locations for relaxation. From the sun-bathed beaches of Thailand's Phuket to the unique scenery of Tibet, China.

Or on a journey of discovery to Malaysia's Kuching and Penang, and beyond to the ski-fields (滑雪场). Holiday Inn makes it easy to relax.

So does the American Express Card. It is the foremost business traveler companion. With no preset spending limit you can spend as much as you have shown us you can afford. You have the flexibility to quickly change your travel plans plus the spending power to make the most of your last minute holiday.

Relax with confidence. Just one of the many benefits of being an American Express Card member and staying at Holiday Inn.

An Advertisement

Items advertised:

- Holiday Inn

- American Express Card

Number of Holiday Inn hotels worldwide: 1) _____

Services offered by Holiday Inn:

- best 2) _____ facilities

- best 3) _____ for relaxation

Advantages of American Express Card:

- no preset 4) _____

- flexibility in changing one's 5) _____

Reading for Fun

An Ad

After a beautiful purebred puppy wandered onto our back porch and made himself at home, my husband composed an ad for the "Lost and Found" column of the local newspaper. It read: "A puppy, male, approximately nine months old, no collar, very friendly, found on Rockbridge Road."

I feared all the details might encourage an unscrupulous person to claim the dog. As I methodically explained why each clue revealed too much, my husband dutifully crossed out the words. Finally, in frustration, he rewrote the ad, reducing it to a single sentence that I couldn't refute.

It read: "Guess what I found?"

Unit 2
Great Perseverance

Passage A   A Brother's Song

Like any good mom, when Karen found out that another baby was on the way, she did what she could to help her 3-year-old son, Michael, prepare for a new sibling.

They found out that the new baby was going to be a girl, and day after day, night after night, Michael sang to his sister in mommy's tummy. He was building a bond of love with his little sister before he even met her.

The pregnancy progressed normally for Karen. In time, the labor pains came. Soon it was every five minutes, every three...every minute. But serious complications arose during delivery and Karen found herself in hours of labor. Would a caesarean section be required? Finally, after a long struggle, Michael's little sister was born. But she was in a very serious condition.

With a siren howling in the night, the ambulance rushed the infant to the neonatal intensive care unit at St. Mary's Hospital, Knoxville Tennessee. The days inched by. The little girl got worse. The pediatrician diagnosed and had to tell the parents "There is very little hope. Be prepared for the worst."

Karen and her husband contacted a local cemetery about a burial plot. They had fixed up a special room in their house for their new baby but now they found themselves having to plan for a funeral. Michael, however, kept begging his parents to let him see his sister. "I want to sing to her," he kept saying.

Week two in intensive care. It looked as if a funeral would come before the week was over. Michael kept nagging about singing to his sister, but kids are never allowed in the intensive care unit. Karen made up her mind, though. She would take Michael whether they liked it or not! If he didn't see his sister right then, he may never see her alive. She dressed him in an oversized suit and marched him into ICU. He looked like a walking laundry basket. But the head nurse recognized him as a child and shouted, "Get that kid out of here now! No children are allowed in ICU."

The mother instinct rose up strong in Karen, and the usually mild-mannered lady glared steel-eyed right into the head nurse's face, her lips a firm line, and said earnestly, "He is not leaving until he sings to his sister!"

Then Karen towed Michael to his sister's bedside. He gazed at the tiny infant losing the battle to live. After a moment, he began to sing. In the pure-hearted voice of a 3-year-old, Michael sang: "You are my sunshine, my only sunshine, you make me happy when skies are gray..."

Instantly the baby girl seemed to respond. The pulse rate began to calm down and became steady. "Keep on singing, Michael," encouraged Karen with tears in her eyes.

"You never know, dear, how much I love you, please don't take my sunshine away..."

As Michael sang to his sister, the baby's ragged, strained breathing became as smooth as a kitten's purr.

"Keep on singing, sweetheart."

"The other night, dear, as I lay sleeping, I dreamed I held you in my arms..." Michael's little sister began to relax as rest, healing rest, seemed to sweep over her.

"Keep on singing, Michael." Tears had now conquered the face of the bossy head nurse. Karen glowed.

"You are my sunshine, my only sunshine. Please don't take my sunshine away..."

The next day...the very next day...the little girl was well enough to go home! *Woman's Day Magazine* called it "The Miracle of a Brother's Song". The medical staff just called it a miracle. Karen called it a miracle of brother's love!

New Words

1. bond	*n.*	（因共同利益或感情而使人连系起来的）纽带
2. bossy	*a.*	爱发号施令的，专横的
3. cemetery	*n.*	墓地，公墓
4. complications	*n.*	并发症
5. conquer	*v.*	征服，占领
6. delivery	*n.*	分娩
7. earnestly	*ad.*	认真地，郑重其事地
8. funeral	*n.*	葬礼，出殡
9. glow	*v.*	（因运动或强烈情感）面部发红发热
10. howl	*v.*	尖叫，啸鸣
11. inch	*v.*	（使）缓慢移动
12. infant	*n.*	婴儿，幼儿
13. instantly	*ad.*	立即，马上
14. intensive	*a.*	集中的，加强的

15. miracle	*n.*	奇迹
16. nag	*v.*	唠叨，跟……纠缠不休
17. plot	*n.*	一块墓地
18. pregnancy	*n.*	怀孕，孕期
19. sibling	*n.*	兄弟姐妹
20. siren	*n.*	汽笛，警报器
21. staff	*n.*	员工，全体职工
22. steady	*a.*	平稳的，稳定的
23. strained	*a.*	不自然的，紧张的
24. tow	*v.*	拖，拉，拽
25. tummy	*n.*	肚子（尤为儿语）

Ⓝotes

1. The pregnancy progressed normally for Karen. In time, the labor pains came. Soon it was every five minutes, every three...every minute.

   凯伦的妊娠进展正常，产前阵痛按期到来了。很快，阵痛密集到每间隔5分钟、3分钟甚至每隔1分钟就有一次。

2. With a siren howling in the night, the ambulance rushed the infant to the neonatal intensive care unit at St. Mary's Hospital, Knoxville Tennessee.

   警笛声划破了深夜的寂静，救护车将婴儿紧急送往田纳西州诺克斯维尔市圣玛丽医院的新生儿重症监护病房。

   neonatal intensive care unit: 新生儿重症监护病房。intensive care unit的缩写是ICU，即重症监护病房。neonatal是个合成词 (compound word)，neo-是前缀 (prefix)，意为"新的"；natal作为医学术语，解释为"出生的"，所以neonatal的意思就是"新生的"。其他由neo-构成的合成词还有neoclassicalism（新古典主义），neocolonialism（新殖民主义）等。

3. They had fixed up a special room in their house for their new baby but now they found themselves having to plan for a funeral.

   他们已经在家里为这个刚出生的孩子专门布置了一个房间，但现在他们却发现自己不得不为这个孩子的葬礼做准备。

   fix up: 收拾，修理，装饰。例如，I'm going to fix up the guest bedroom before my mother-in-law arrives.

   find oneself doing sth.: 发现自己不知不觉地或没有预先计划地在做某事，例如，Peter, who was usually shy, found himself talking to the girls.

4. She dressed him in an oversized suit and marched him into ICU. He looked like a walking laundry basket.

她给迈克穿上了一件超大的外套，然后领着他径直朝重症监护病房走去。他看上去就像是一个正在行走的洗衣筐。

march sb. (into): 使前进，使行进。例如，The teacher marched the children out to the playground. march在文中还包含有"毅然，带着决心向前走"的意思。

5. The mother instinct rose up strong in Karen, and the usually mild-mannered lady glared steel-eyed right into the head nurse's face, her lips a firm line, and said earnestly, "He is not leaving until he sings to his sister!"

凯伦身上的母性迸发了出来，那位平素举止文雅，态度温和的女士此刻目光坚定地看着护士长的脸，嘴唇抿成一条坚毅的弧线，郑重其事地说："没有给他妹妹唱歌，他是不会离开的。"

Ⓔxercises

1. Choose the best answer.

1) Why did Michael sing to his younger sister while she was still in mommy's tummy?

A. Because he'd like to do some preparatory work for his new sibling.

B. Because he was very pleased that the new baby was going to be a girl.

C. Because he wanted to build a bond of love with his little sister.

D. Because he wanted to relieve mommy's labor pains.

2) Why did Karen and her husband contact a local cemetery?

A. Because they had to fix up a burial plot for their dying daughter.

B. Because they gave up hope for their little daughter.

C. Because their little daughter was in a hopeless condition.

D. Because there were not sufficient intensive care units.

3) Karen dressed Michael in an oversized suit because _____.

A. she wanted the medical staff to like Michael

B. kids are not allowed in intensive care units

C. Michael kept nagging about singing to his sister

D. the head nurse didn't like Michael

4) How did the head nurse respond when she recognized Michael as a child?

A. She was amused as Michael looked funny in an oversized suit.

B. She laughed as Michael looked like a walking laundry basket.

C. She sympathized with the family and felt sorry for Michael.

D. She was very angry and determined to get the kid out.

5) Why did Karen glare-steel-eyed right into the head nurse's face?

    A. Because Karen always behaved in bad manners.

    B. Because Karen knew this might be the last time for Michael to see his sister alive.

    C. Because Karen was very angry as the head nurse shouted at her son.

    D. Because Karen was disappointed with the head nurse's work.

2. Complete the statements that follow the questions.

1) How was Michael's little sister when she was born?

    She was in _____.

2) Which department of the hospital admits the newly born infants who are seriously ill?

    The neonatal _____.

3) How was the baby girl when Michael first saw her?

    The tiny infant was losing the _____.

4) How did the baby girl respond when she heard Michael singing?

    Her pulse rate began to _____.

5) How did the head nurse respond when she saw Michael's singing worked?

    _____.

3. Match the following words with the definitions below and then fill in the blanks with their proper forms.

instantly	diagnose	steady	conquer	bond
healing	gaze	intensive	funeral	complication
earnestly	staff	miracle	nag	delivery

1) (*noun*) sth. that unites two or more people, such as love or a shared interest; link or tie

    The trade agreement helped to strengthen the _____ of friendship between the two countries.

2) (*noun*) sth. that makes a medical condition more dangerous or difficult to treat

    Some patients develop _____ after surgery.

3) (*noun*) the process of giving birth to a child

    Mrs. Smith had a relatively easy _____.

4) (*verb*) to frequently ask sb. to do sth. they do not want to do

    The kids are always _____ me for new toys.

5) (*noun*) a ceremony for burying or burning a dead person

"You are going to fail your exams if you don't work hard." "That's my _____, not yours."

6) (*verb*) to take possession of (sth.) by force

Computers can only do what they're told to do. They will not _____ human beings.

7) (*noun*) sth. lucky that you did not expect to happen or did not think was possible

It's really a _____ that he wasn't killed in that car crash!

8) (*adjective*) concentrating all one's efforts on a specific area

They teach you English in an _____ course lasting just a week.

9) (*adjective*) staying at the same level, speed, value etc.

She listened to the _____ rhythm of his breathing as he slept.

10) (*noun*) the people who work for an organization, especially a school or business

It's a small hospital with a _____ of just over a hundred.

11) (*verb*) to look at sb. or sth. for a long time, giving it all your attention often without realizing you are doing so

He lay on the bed _____ up at the ceiling.

12) (*verb*) to find out the nature of sth. (especially an illness) by observing its symptoms

The book _____ our present economic ills.

13) (*adverb*) seriously, not jokingly

I _____ beg you to reconsider your decision.

14) (*adjective*) making sb. feel better after they have been ill or unhappy

The hot springs are known to have excellent _____ power.

15) (*adverb*) without delay, immediately

His voice was _____ recognizable.

Reading Skills

Recognizing References

指代

在一篇英语阅读文章中，常常会出现几个人物，几件物品或几件事情。如果在一个句子或段落中反复使用同一个人名、物名、地名，文章读起来就会累赘拗口。为了避免出现这种情况，作者通常会用代词来表示文中已出现的相应的人名、地名、物名。这种现象叫做"指代"。

指代的作用是使句子、段落及文章结构紧凑，意思简明，但同时也带来了要清楚指代关系的问题。假如在一篇文章中同时出现两个或以上的事件、人物（尤其是同一性别），我们就会遇到多个指代关系。这时，就需要我们仔细分析，了解每一个指代所表示的内容，否则，就会产生歧义，造成理解失误，答题错误。

[例] Jane was a school teacher. Not long ago, she (1) went through a short time of depression. She (2) was always in low spirits and fell behind in all her (3) work. Her (4) best friend Mary sensed her (5) change and one day pulled her (6) aside and asked what was wrong with her (7). Jane asked Mary not to worry about her (8) and said that she (9) could solve the problem all by herself (10). Mary invited Jane to go for a walk with her (11) and talked about what was going on in Jane's life. She (12) helped Jane to figure out what she (13) wanted to do. Finally, Jane found one way out of her (14) depression. Later, she (15) said she (16) didn't know what would have happened if Mary hadn't helped her (17).

段落开始部分Jane was a school teacher. Not long ago, she (1) went through a short time of depression. She (2) was always in low spirits and fell behind in all her (3) work. 介绍了Jane 的情况。在这三句话中，只有一个人物，所以我们可以清楚地知道两个人称代词she（1）和（2），都是指代Jane。

从段落的中间部分开始，又出现了另一个人物Mary，而且和Jane 是同一性别。我们阅读时应细心辨别。

Her (4) best friend Mary sensed her (5) change and one day pulled her (6) aside and asked what was wrong with her (7). 她（4）最好的朋友Mary 察觉到了她（5）的变化，有一天把她（6）拉到一边，问她（7）怎么了。从句子意思分析，前两个物主代词（4）和（5）都是指代Jane。从上下文我们知道是Mary把Jane拉到一边问Jane 是怎么回事，所以后两个人称代词（6）和（7）同样都指代Jane。

Jane asked Mary not to worry about her (8) and said that she (9) could solve the problem all by herself (10). Jane 叫Mary不要担心她（8），说她（9）会自己（10）解决这个问题。人称代词（8）的指代很明显，指的是Jane，因为问题出在Jane身上，而不在Mary身上，解决自身问题的只能是Jane。所以，（9）和（10）同样指的是Jane。

Mary invited Jane to go for a walk with her (11) and talked about what was going on in Jane's life. Mary邀请Jane和她（11）一起去散步，一起谈谈Jane的生活中发生了什么事。Jane 散步的同伴是Mary，因此（11）指代 Mary。

She (12) helped Jane to figure out what she (13) wanted to do. 她（12）帮助Jane 明白了她（13）要做什么。是Mary帮助Jane，根据上下文，我们可以清楚地看出（12）指代Mary，（13）指代Jane。

Later, she (15) said she (16) didn't know what would have happened if Mary hadn't helped her (17). 后来，她（15）说假如没有Mary帮助她（17），她（16）不知道自己会发生什么事。从上下文可以清楚地看出，（15）、（16）、（17）都是指代Jane。

Exercises

1. Read the following paragraph and recognize the references.

Dewey was a crazy rock'n'roll guitar player in a band. He decided to ask Zack, another talented guitarist of the band, to develop a rock song. So he 1) encouraged him 2) to write his 3) first song in his 4) life. Zack had never written any song before. He 5) was afraid he 6) couldn't live up to Dewey's expectations, but he 7) was determined to do his 8) utmost to do it well. After some time, he 9) beautifully finished composing the song. Dewey and his band loved it very much, so he 10) decided to play the song in the Battle of Bands. The song turned out to be a huge success and made Zack feel it was worthy of his 11) hard work. Dewey thanked his 12) good friend and embraced him 13) with excitement. On the audience's request, Dewey and his 14) band gave an encore—a song Dewey wrote by himself 15).

1) _____ 2) _____ 3) _____ 4) _____ 5) _____
6) _____ 7) _____ 8) _____ 9) _____ 10) _____
11) _____ 12) _____ 13) _____ 14) _____ 15) _____

2. Read the following paragraph and recognize the references.

People have kept a lot of records of their various hobbies since they 1) began to take them 2) up. Hobbies are important to people because they 3) can provide them with knowledge and relaxation and help them 4) relieve stress and unhappiness. They 5) can be pursued by anyone, men or women, old or young, rich or poor. The cavemen were the first creative hobbyists we know. They 6) found fun in having hobbies in the free time they had after the hunting and fighting. Nowadays, people have more leisure time than they 7) had in the past. Interesting hobbies can be the best way for them 8) to solve the problems of how to use it 9). The hobbies people choose may be the ones 10) that will keep them 11) interested all their lives. But sometimes, people may outgrow their hobbies and it is necessary for them 12) to choose another 13). Whatever the hobby they choose, it is good if it 14) keeps them 15) busy and happy.

1) _____   2) _____   3) _____   4) _____   5) _____

6) _____   7) _____   8) _____   9) _____   10) _____

11) _____   12) _____   13) _____   14) _____   15) _____

Passage B   Ask, Ask, Ask

Read the passage and judge whether the following statements are true (T) or false (F).

1) Markita discovered the secret of selling when she was seven years old.

2) Markita was awfully shy before she began selling Girl Scouts cookies.

3) Markita's father abandoned Markita and her mother when she was 13 years old.

4) Markita and her mother shared the dream of traveling around the world.

5) Markita's aunt advised Markita to dress professionally and rightly when doing business.

6) Markita starred in a Disney movie that was about her adventure.

7) Markita also wrote a bestseller single-handedly.

8) Markita thinks everyone is selling something everyday and everywhere except in school.

9) The toughest selling challenge for Markita was to sell Girl Scout cookies to a federal warden on live TV.

10) Markita failed to persuade the warden to buy some Girl Scout cookies.

The greatest saleswoman in the world today doesn't mind if you call her a girl. That's because Markita Andrews has generated more than eighty thousand dollars selling Girl Scout (女童子军) cookies since she was seven years old.

Going door-to-door after school, the painfully shy Markita transformed herself into a cookie-selling dynamo (精力充沛的人) when she discovered, at age 13, the secret of selling.

It starts with desire. Burning, white-hot desire.

For Markita and her mother, who worked as a waitress in New York after her husband left them when Markita was eight years old, their dream was to travel the globe. "I'll work hard to make enough money to send you to college," her mother said one day. "You'll go to college and when you graduate, you'll make enough money to take you and me around the world. Okay?"

So at age 13 when Markita read in her Girl Scout magazine that the Scout who sold the most cookies

would win an all-expenses-paid trip for two around the world, she decided to sell all the Girl Scout cookies she could—more Girl Scout cookies than anyone else in the world, ever.

But desire alone is not enough. To make her dream come true, Markita knew she needed a plan.

"Always wear your right outfit (全套服装), your professional garb (服装)," her aunt advised. "When you are doing business, dress like you are doing business. Wear your Girl Scout uniform. When you go up to people in their tenement (廉价公寓) buildings at 4:30 or 6:30 and especially on Friday night, ask for a big order. Always smile, whether they buy or not, always be nice. And don't ask them to buy your cookies; ask them to invest."

Lots of other Scouts may have wanted that trip around the world. Lots of other Scouts may have had a plan. But only Markita went off in her uniform each day after school, ready to ask—and keep asking—folks to invest in her dream. "Hi, I have a dream. I'm earning a trip around the world for me and my mom by merchandising (销售) Girl Scout cookies," she'd say at the door. "Would you like to invest in one dozen or two dozen boxes of cookies?"

Markita sold 3,526 boxes of Girl Scout cookies that year and won her trip around the world. Since then, she has sold more than 42,000 boxes of Girl Scout cookies, spoken at sales conventions across the country, starred in a Disney movie about her adventure and co-authored the bestseller, *How to Sell More Cookies, Condos, Cadillacs, Computers...And Everything Else*.

Markita is no smarter and no more extroverted (外向的) than thousands of other people, young and old, with dreams of their own. The difference is Markita had discovered the secret of selling: Ask, Ask, Ask! Many people fail before they even begin because they fail to ask for what they want. The fear of rejection (拒绝) leads many of us to reject ourselves and our dreams long before anyone else ever has the chance—no matter what we're selling.

And everyone is selling something. "You're selling yourself every day—in school, to your boss, to new people you meet," said Markita at 14. "My mother is a waitress: she sells the daily special. Mayors and presidents trying to get votes are selling...I see selling everywhere I look. Selling is part of the whole world."

It takes courage to ask for what you want. Courage is not the absence of fear. It's doing the right things despite one's fear. And, as Markita has discovered, the more you ask, the easier (and more fun) it gets.

Once, on live TV, the producer decided to give Markita her toughest selling challenge. Markita was asked to sell Girl Scout cookies to another guest on the show. "Would you like to invest in one dozen or two dozen boxes of Girl Scout cookies?" she asked.

"Girl Scout cookies? I don't buy any Girl Scout cookies!" he replied. "I'm a Federal Penitentiary (重罪监狱) warden (监狱长). I put 2,000 rapists, robbers, criminals, muggers and child abusers to bed every night."

Unruffled (镇定的，沉着的), Markita quickly countered, "Mister, if you take some of these cookies, maybe you won't be so mean and angry and evil. And, mister, I think it would be a good idea for you to take some of these cookies back for every one of your 2,000 prisoners, too."

Markita asked.

The warden wrote a check.

Reading Comprehension from PRETCO

Task 1

Directions: *After reading the following passage, you will find 5 questions or unfinished statements. For each question or statement there are 4 choices marked A, B, C and D. You should make the correct choice and mark the corresponding letter with a single line through the center. (2006. 06)*

When a rare disease ALD threatened to kill the four-year-old boy Lorenzo, his parents refused to give up hope. Doctors explained that there was no cure for ALD, and that he would probably die within three years. But Lorenzo's parents set out to prove the doctors wrong.

The parents devoted themselves to keeping their son alive and searching for a cure. But doctors and the families of other ALD patients often refused to take them seriously. They thought the efforts to find a cure were a waste of time, and drug companies weren't interested in supporting research into such a rare disease.

However, the parents still refused to give up and spent every available hour in medical libraries and talked to anyone who would help. Through trial and error (反复试验), they finally created a cure from ingredients (调料) commonly found in the kitchen. The cure, named "Lorenzo's Oil", saved the boy's life. Despite the good result, scientists and doctors remained unconvinced. They said there was no real evidence that the oil worked and that the treatment was just a theory. As a result, some families with ALD children were reluctant to try it.

Finally, the boy's father organized an international study to test the oil. After ten years of trials, the answer is: the oil keeps ALD children healthy.

1) Doctors said that Lorenzo might die within three years because _____.

    A. they had never treated the disease before

    B. Lorenzo was too young to be cured

    C. no cure had been found for ALD

    D. ALD was a rare disease

2) The families of other ALD patients thought that _____.

    A. the research for the new cure would cost too much money

    B. the efforts of Lorenzo's parents were a waste of time

    C. Lorenzo's parents would succeed in finding a cure

    D. Lorenzo's Oil was a real cure for ALD

3) Scientists and doctors believed that Lorenzo's Oil _____.

    A. was really effective

    B. was a success story

    C. only worked in theory

    D. would save the boy's life

4) Lorenzo's father organized an international study to _____.

    A. test Lorenzo's Oil

    B. get financial support

    C. find a cure for the disease

    D. introduce the cure worldwide

5) From the passage we can conclude that _____.

    A. doctors remain doubtful of the effectiveness of the cure

    B. many ALD patients still refuse to use the oil

    C. various cures have been found for ALD

    D. the oil really works as a cure for ALD

Task 2

Directions: *After reading the following passage, you will find 5 questions or unfinished statements. For each question or statement there are 4 choices marked A, B, C and D. You should make the correct choice and mark the corresponding letter with a single line through the center. (2002. 12)*

There are some problem areas for international students and immigrants studying in the United States. Making friends is a challenge (this is also true for some American students). Many colleges and universities offer a variety of student clubs and organizations where both foreign-born and native American students have a greater chance of meeting people with shared interests. Information about these out-of-class activities is often posted in the student center and listed in the student newspaper. Sometimes foreign students and immigrant students find Americans to be "cliquish" (有派性的). (Americans find some none-US-born students do be cliquish as well.) If people feel separated from the social aspects of American college life, they should actively seek people with shared interests. It's unlikely that students will make friends just by passing people on the campus.

Foreign or immigrant students may feel confused during the first few weeks at a new school because they do not understand the system and are not willing to ask questions. Many students do not take advantage of the numerous services offered on campus that assist students in developing new skills and social groups. Some colleges offer students tutorial (辅导的) support in such subjects as writing, language study, computer skills, and other basic subjects. Students who appear to be most successful in "learning the ropes" are those who can solve problems by taking the initiative to ask questions, locate resources, and experience new social situations.

1) In the United States, students can find friends with the same interests by _____.
   A. making friends on the campus
   B. reading the student newspaper
   C. visiting the student center
   D. joining the student clubs

2) The sentence "…people feel separated from the social aspects of American college life…" (Lines 7—8, Para.1) means they have difficulty in _____.
   A. joining social activities within the campus
   B. being easily accepted by the university
   C. finding people with shared interests
   D. getting a job in American society

3) When they first come to colleges, some foreign students may feel confused because _____.
   A. they are denied any help from people around
   B. they are provided with new services
   C. they are faced with an unfamiliar educational system
   D. they are unwilling to adapt themselves to the new environment

4) The phrase "learning the ropes" (Line 6, Para. 2) is closest in meaning to _____.
   A. finding the way to develop new skills
   B. having the skills to make conversations
   C. learning how to answer questions
   D. knowing how to handle problems

5) From the passage we may conclude that foreign students _____.
   A. may face some problems in adjusting to college life
   B. are unlikely to be successful in American college life

C. are not good at developing friendship and social groups

D. can hardly learn well when they enter an American college

Reading for Fun

Mow Lawns for Free

A Coon Rapids (库恩雷佩兹市) man who has struggled to lose weight is hoping a lawn mower (割草机) will help him shed between 20 and 50 pounds. After working up quite a sweat mowing his own lawn this summer, Darrell Nelson thought that he could get a good workout by mowing lawns for other people as well. So, on the Website Craigslist, he placed an ad offering to mow lawns for free. He thinks if he mows a lawn per day nearly every day of the week, he will be able to keep an exercise program going. He said he has a hard time keeping commitments to himself, but he will stick to commitments he makes to others. "This is no joke or gimmick," he wrote on the Web. "I need to lose weight. I have struggled on sticking to my exercise programs, including just walking, for quite a while now."

Nelson is a former weightlifer (举重运动员) who's about 5-foot-9 and 258 pounds. Since news of his ad spread, he has received calls from the media, strangers—even some women who have asked him out on dates. "My life has been turned upside down, man, unbelievable," he said. "I was planning on doing five lawns: mine plus four others. Now, I'm doing six lawns: mine plus five others...I was just trying to do some yards and lose some weight, and it just—see there—away it went."

Unit 3
Going into the UN

Passage A   History of the United Nations

The name "United Nations", coined by Franklin D. Roosevelt, the 32nd President of the United States, was first used in the Declaration by United Nations of 1 January 1942, during the Second World War, when representatives of 26 nations pledged their governments to continue fighting together against the Axis Powers.

States first established international organizations to cooperate on specific matters. The International Telecommunication Union was founded in 1865 as the International Telegraph Union, and the Universal Postal Union was established in 1874. Both are now the specialized agencies of the United Nations.

In 1899, the first International Peace Conference was held in The Hague to elaborate instruments for settling crises peacefully, preventing wars and codifying rules of warfare. It adopted the Convention for the Peaceful Settlement of International Disputes and established the Permanent Court of Arbitration, which began to work in 1902.

The forerunner of the United Nations was the League of Nations, an organization conceived in similar circumstances during the First World War, and established in 1919 under the Treaty of Versailles "to promote international cooperation and to achieve peace and security".

The International Labor Organization was also created under the Treaty of Versailles as an affiliated agency of the League. The League of Nations ceased its activities after failing to prevent the Second World War.

In 1945, representatives of 50 countries met in San Francisco at the UN Conference on International Organization to draw up the Charter of the United Nations. Those delegates deliberated on the basis of proposals worked out by the representatives of China, the Soviet Union, the United Kingdom and the United States at Dumbarton Oaks in August-October 1944. The Charter was signed on 26

June 1945 by the representatives of the 50 countries. Poland, which was not represented at the Conference, signed it later and became one of the original 51 member states.

The United Nations officially came into existence on 24 October 1945, when the Charter had been ratified by China, France, the Soviet Union, the United Kingdom, the United States and a majority of other signatories. United Nations Day is celebrated on 24 October each year.

The Aims of the United Nations:

To keep peace throughout the world.

To develop friendly relations between nations.

To work together to help people live better lives, to eliminate poverty, disease and illiteracy in the world, to stop environmental destruction and to encourage respect for each other's rights and freedoms.

To be a centre for helping nations achieve these aims.

The Principles of the United Nations:

All Member States have sovereign equality.

All Member States must obey the Charter.

Countries must try to settle their differences by peaceful means.

Countries must avoid using force or threatening to use force.

The UN may not interfere in the domestic affairs of any country.

Countries should try to assist the United Nations.

New Words

1. affiliated	*a.*	隶属的，附属的	
2. arbitration	*n.*	仲裁，公断	
3. charter	*n.*	宪章，规章	
4. codify	*v.*	把（法律、条例、事实等）编集成典	
5. coin	*v.*	创造，杜撰	
6. conceive	*v.*	设想，构想	
7. convention	*n.*	公约，协定	
8. crisis	*n.*	危机	
9. deliberate	*v.*	商讨	
10. dispute	*n.*	争端，纠纷	
11. domestic	*a.*	本国的，国内的	
12. elaborate	*v.*	详细制定	

13. eliminate	*v.*	消除，清除
14. forerunner	*n.*	先驱，先导
15. illiteracy	*n.*	文盲
16. interfere	*v.*	干预，干涉
17. permanent	*a.*	永久的，长久的
18. pledge	*v.*	保证，发誓
19. ratify	*v.*	正式批准
20. representative	*n.*	代表
21. signatory	*n.*	签署者，缔约国
22. sovereign	*a.*	有主权的，完全独立的
23. threaten	*v.*	威胁，恐吓
24. treaty	*n.*	条约，协定
25. warfare	*n.*	战争，冲突

Notes

1. the United Nations: 联合国（UN）有六个主要机构：大会、安全理事会、经济及社会理事会、托管理事会、国际法院和秘书处。

   联合国大会：简称"联大"，由全体会员国组成，它是联合国的审议机构。

   联合国安全理事会：简称"安理会"，现由中国、法国、俄罗斯、英国、美国5个常任理事国和10个非常任理事国组成。

   联合国经济及社会理事会：是协调14个联合国专门机构、10个职司委员会和5个区域委员会的经济、社会和相关工作的主要机构。

   联合国托管理事会：由安理会的五个常任理事国组成，随着联合国最后一块托管领土帕劳取得独立，理事会于1994年11月1日正式停止运作。

   国际法院：是联合国的主要司法机关，目标是实现联合国的一项主要宗旨："以和平方法且依正义及国际法原则，调整或解决足以破坏和平的国际争端或情势"。

   秘书处：联合国秘书处是联合国的行政秘书事务机构。秘书长是联合国的行政官，担任重大的国际政治责任。秘书长由联合国大会和安理会推荐，任期5年。

2. the International Telecommunication Union: 国际电信联盟

   the International Telegraph Union: 国际电报联盟

   the Universal Postal Union: 万国邮政联盟

3. In 1899, the first International Peace Conference was held in The Hague to elaborate instruments for settling crises peacefully, preventing wars and codifying rules of warfare.

   1899年，为了和平解决危机，预防战争和编纂战争法则，第一届国际和平会议在海牙举行。

   The Hague: 海牙，荷兰西部城市，是该国王宫，政府机构所在地，联合国国际法院等机构也设于此地。

4. Those delegates deliberated on the basis of proposals worked out by the representatives of China, the Soviet Union, the United Kingdom and the United States at Dumbarton Oaks in August-October 1944.

代表们在中国、苏联、英国和美国四国代表于1944年8月至10月在美国顿巴顿橡树园会议上提出的提案基础上进行了讨论。

the United Kingdom: the United Kingdom of Great Britain and Northern Ireland, 大不列颠及北爱尔兰联合王国，即英国。

Dumbarton Oaks: 美国顿巴顿橡树园。1944年8月至10月，中苏美英四国代表在美国顿巴顿橡树园举行会议，草拟了"联合国"机构的组织方案。

Exercises

1. Choose the best answer.

1) What is the relationship between the United Nations and the League of Nations?

A. The League of Nations is a specialized agency of the United Nations.

B. The United Nations belongs to the League of Nations.

C. The League of Nations is the predecessor to the United Nations.

D. None of the above.

2) Which of the following events happened first?

A. The Charter of the United Nations was drew up.

B. The first International Peace Conference was held in The Hague.

C. The International Telecommunication Union was founded.

D. The League of Nations was established.

3) Which of the following statements is TRUE according to the reading text?

A. The United Nations officially came into existence when the Charter had been ratified by all the signatories.

B. The League of Nations ceased its activities after failing to prevent the First World War.

C. United Nations Day is celebrated every two years.

D. The League of Nations and the International Labor Organization were established under the same treaty.

4) Which of the following countries was NOT represented at the UN Conference to draw up the Charter of the United Nations?

A. The Soviet Union.

B. The United Kingdom.

C. The United States.

D. Poland.

5) What is the aim of the first International Peace Conference?

A. To settle crises peacefully and to follow firmly the Treaty of Versailles.

B. To codify rules of warfare and to sign the Charter of the United Nations.

C. To prevent wars, to develop friendly relations between countries and to settle disputes peacefully.

D. To settle crises peacefully, to codify rules of warfare and to prevent wars.

2. Complete the statements that follow the questions.

1) Who created the name "United Nations"?

It was coined by _____.

2) Where was the first International Peace Conference held?

It was held in _____.

3) How many countries signed the Charter of the United Nations?

_____ signed the Charter of the United Nations.

4) According to the principles of the United Nations, how should countries settle their differences?

Countries must try to settle their differences _____.

5) According to the principles of the United Nations, what right did not the UN have?

The UN has no right to _____.

3. Match the following words with the definitions below and then fill in the blanks with their proper forms.

permanent	deliberate	elaborate	circumstance	interfere
threaten	dispute	specialize	cease	represent
original	delegate	agency	domestic	adopt

1) (*adjective*) lasting for a long time

The injury left him with a _____ limp.

2) (*noun*) a situation in which two countries or groups of people quarrel or disagree with each other

The two countries have had a _____ about the border for a long time.

3) (*noun*) someone who has been elected or chosen to speak, vote, or take decisions for a group

The conference was attended by _____ from five countries.

4) (*adjective*) existing at the beginning of a particular period

Years have passed by, but the garden still has many of its _____ features.

5) (*verb*) to think about or discuss sth. very carefully, especially before you make an important decision

They met to _____ on possible solutions to the problem.

6) (*verb*) to say that you will hurt sb., if you do not get what you want

The attacker _____ the policeman with a gun, but the latter was not afraid at all.

7) (*verb*) to give more details or information about sth.

He said he had evidence, but refused to _____ further.

8) (*verb*) to stop sth. from happening or continuing

The two armed forces were asked to _____ fire and get down to negotiation.

9) (*verb*) to decide to start using a particular idea, plan, or method

The country _____ a series of new policies to accelerate (加速) its economic development.

10) (*verb*) to give special or particular attention to; major in

He _____ in law at college for his ambition of being a lawyer in the future.

11) (*noun*) an organization or department, especially within a government

Central Intelligence _____ is the department of the US government that collects information about other countries secretly.

12) (*adjective*) of or inside a particular country

You go to the same terminal for _____ and international flights.

13) (*verb*) to speak or act officially for another person, group, or organization

The 2008 Beijing Olympic Games and Paralympic Games attracted a large number of contestants _____ more than two hundred countries and regions.

14) (*noun*) the conditions that are connected with a situation

Please believe me that I will not give up in any _____.

15) (*verb*) to get involved in a situation without the right to do so or being invited to do so

I want my father to stop _____ with my personal affairs and let me decide by myself.

Reading Skills

Ⓢcanning
查读

查读是带着具体的问题跳跃式浏览全文，其目的在于捕获某一特定信息，如人名、地点、日期、某个事件或某种数据等等。查读是一种有选择性的阅读，因此，为了获取所需要的具体信息，在阅读过程中要忽略与问题无关的内容。查读的特点是"见木不见林"。查读时通常可以按照以下步骤来进行：

1) 明确要查找的具体细节，比如确定要查找的是人名、地点、时间还是事件。

2) 在了解待查信息的基础上，可预先估计其可能出现的形式。例如，人名和地点的第一个字母通常是大写，日期经常用数字表示。这些有效的推测都可以帮助读者以最快的速度找到相关信息。

3) 熟悉阅读材料常见的组织形式。例如电话簿、参考书目等通常是按照字母顺序排列的。历史资料和文献一般是按照年、月、日顺序排列。电视节目单则根据时间和频道排列。

4) 根据阅读材料的组织形式，在阅读材料中迅速地确定最有可能包含待查信息的具体位置。例如，要从世界城市天气状况一览表中查找"Rome"的天气情况，"Rome"就是最为关键的线索词。根据地名一般按字母顺序排列的规律，读者应该直接到以字母"R"开头的城市中寻找。

5) 在找到线索词所处的具体位置之后，读者应当仔细阅读这一部分，确定该部分的内容是否包含自己要找的答案。

此外，为了有效查读，提高阅读效率，读者可以根据阅读材料的不同排列方式采用不同的眼部运动。对行距较短的柱状排列方式，如电话簿、书目等可采用从上至下的垂直阅读方式；而对行距跨度较大的篇章排列方式则可使用Z型的眼部运动来进行有效的查读。

[例] Holidaymakers who are bored with baking beaches and overheated hotel rooms head for a big igloo. Swedish businessman Nile Bergqvist is delighted with his new hotel, the world's first igloo hotel. Built in a small town in Lapland, it has been attracting lots of visitors, but soon the fun will be over.

In two weeks' time Bergqvist's ice creation will be nothing more than a pool of water. "We don't see it as a big problem," he says. "We just look forward to replacing it."

Bergqvist built his first igloo in 1991 for an art exhibition. It was so successful that he designed the present one, which measures roughly 200 square meters. Six workmen spent more than eight weeks piling 1,000 tons of snow onto a wooden base; when the snow froze, the base was removed. "The only wooden thing we have left in the igloo is the front door," he says.

After their stay, all visitors receive a survival certificate recording their success. With no windows, nowhere to hang clothes and temperatures below 0℃, it may seem more like a survival test than a relaxing hotel break. "It's great fun," Bergqvist explains, "as well as a good start in survival training."

The popularity of the igloo is beyond doubt: it is now attracting tourists from all over the world. At least 800 people have stayed at the igloo this season even though there are only 10 rooms. "You can get a lot of people in," explains Bergqvist. "The beds are three meters wide by two meters long, and can fit at least four at one time."

1) When the writer says "the fun will be over" (Line 3, Para.1) he refers to the fact that _____.
   A. hotel guests will be frightened at the thought of the hard test
   B. Bergqvist's hotel will soon become a pool of water
   C. holidaymakers will soon get tired of the big igloo
   D. a bigger igloo will replace the present one

2) When guests leave the igloo hotel they will receive a paper stating that _____.
   A. they have visited Lapland   B. they have had an ice-snow holiday
   C. they have had great fun sleeping on ice   D. they have had a taste of adventure

通读文章后，较简单的题目往往能立即解决，但有时会出现一些综合性较强、结构较复杂的试题。如果只看一遍文章，很难回答问题，这时就需要对文章里面的细节、结构、生词的含义进行认真分析、推敲，才能选出正确答案。但若再回头通读全文就会耽误考试时间。我们可以利用查读的方法，对相关词语及句子甚至段落进行研究，从而较快选准答案。

问题1：When the writer says "the fun will be over" he refers to the fact that ____.

我们用查读的方法对所给选项进行分析。本文的目的是给人们介绍igloo（一种因纽特人的住宅），一种新的度假方式。文章最后一段第一句话"The popularity of the igloo is beyond doubt: it is now attracting tourists from all over the world"表达了这种度假方式很受欢迎，许多人都想去试一试。而A选项"客人一想到这种严峻的考验就感到害怕"，C选项"度假的人很快就会对这座冰屋感到厌倦"，和文章表达的意思不符，故首先排除。

以"the fun will be over"为线索进行查读，我们发现第一段最后一句"Built in a small town in Lapland, it has been attracting lots of visitors, but soon the fun will be over"和下段第一句"In two weeks' time Bergqvist's ice creation will be nothing more than a pool of water"与题目相关。理解了这两句话，我们就可以确定选项B为正确答案。

问题2：When guests leave the igloo hotel they will receive a paper stating that ____ .

查读得知，与这个问题相关的句子为第四段第一句"After their stay, all visitors receive a survival certificate recording their success."这句话中的两个单词survival和certificate，可能会造成一点理解上的困难。但我们联系上下文进行推敲，不难发现certificate为一份记录他们成功的paper（文件、证明）。而"成功"意味着两种情况：其一为克服艰巨的困难，把事情办成；其二为在危险的情况下，侥幸取胜。把这两种意义与选项进行对比，我们可以断定D为正确答案。

Exercises

1. Read the following passage and choose the best answer.

Anne Whitney, a sophomore at Colorado State University, first had a problem taking tests when she began college. "I was always well prepared for my tests. Sometimes I studied for weeks before a test. Yet I would go in to take the test, only to find I could not answer the questions correctly. I would blank out because of nervousness and fear. I couldn't think of the answers. My low grades on the tests did not show what I knew to the teacher." Another student in microbiology had similar experiences. He said, "My first chemistry test was very difficult. Then, on the second test, I sat down to take it, and I was so nervous that I was shaking. My hands were moving up and down so quickly that it was hard to hold my pencil. I knew the material and I knew the answers. Yet I couldn't even write them down!"

These two young students were experiencing something called test anxiety. Because a student worries and is uneasy about a test, his or her mind does not work as well as it usually does. The student can not write or think clearly because of the extreme tension and nervousness. Although poor grades are often a result of poor study habits, sometimes test anxiety causes the low grades. Recently, test anxiety had been recognized as a real problem, not just an excuse or a false explanation of lazy students.

Special university counseling courses try to help students. In these courses, counselors try to help students by teaching them how to manage test anxiety. At some universities, students take tests to measure their anxiety. If the tests show their anxiety is high, the students can take short courses to help them deal with their tension. These courses teach students how to relax their bodies. Students are trained to become calm in very tense situations. By controlling their nervousness, they can let their minds work at ease. Learned information then comes out without difficulty on a test.

An expert at the University of California explains, "With almost all students, relaxation and less stress are felt after taking our program. Most of them experience better control during their tests. Almost all have some improvement. With some, the improvement is very great."

    1) To "blank out" is probably _____.

        A. to be like a blanket

        B. to be sure of an answer

        C. to be unable to think clearly

        D. to show knowledge to the teacher

    2) Test anxiety has been recognized as _____.

        A. an excuse for laziness

        B. the result of poor study habits

        C. a real problem

        D. something that cannot be changed

Passage B　The Introduction of UN

Read the passage and judge whether the following statements are true (T) or false (F).

1) The United Nations officially came into existence when the UN Charter had been ratified by all the original 51 member states.

2) In the General Assembly, powerful countries have more voting rights than poor countries.

3) The decisions taken by the General Assembly are binding.

4) The United Nations has its own flag, its own post office and its own postage stamps.

5) In the United Nations, there is only one official language—English.

6) In the UN, all member states have the same rights and obligations.

7) The UN has certain right to interfere in some countries' domestic affairs.

8) Once the United Nations takes actions against a certain country, all the member states are supposed to give no help to that country.

9) The United Nations have several headquarters, two of which are respectively located in New York City and Geneva.

10) The sole essential function of the UN is to maintain international peace and security.

The United Nations officially came into existence on 24 October 1945, when the UN Charter had been ratified by a majority of the original 51 member states. The day is now celebrated each year around the world as United Nations Day.

The purpose of the United Nations is to bring all nations of the world together to work for peace and development, based on the principles of justice, human dignity and the well-being of all people. It affords the opportunity for countries to balance global interdependence and national interests when addressing international problems.

There are currently 192 members of the United Nations. They meet in the General Assembly, which is the closest thing to a world parliament. Each country, large or small, rich or poor, has a single vote. However, none of the decisions taken by the Assembly are binding. Nevertheless, the Assembly's decisions become resolutions that carry the weight of world governmental opinion.

The United Nations Headquarters is in New York City but the land and buildings are international territory. The United Nations has its own flag, its own post office and its own postage stamps. Six official languages are used at the United Nations—Arabic, Chinese, English, French, Russian and Spanish. The UN European Headquarters is in the Palais des Nations, Geneva, Switzerland. It has offices in Vienna, Austria and Economic Commissions in Addis Ababa in Ethiopia, Amman in Jordan,

Bangkok in Thailand and Santiago in Chile. The senior officer of the United Nations Secretariat is the Secretary-General.

The essential functions of the UN are to maintain international peace and security, to develop friendly relations among nations, to cooperate internationally in solving international economic, social, cultural and human problems, to promote respect for human rights and fundamental freedoms and to be a center for coordinating the actions of nations in attaining these common ends.

No country takes precedence over another in the UN. Each member's rights and obligations are the same. All must contribute to the peaceful settlement of international dispute, and members have pledged to refrain from the threat or use of force against other states. The UN has no right to interfere in any state's internal affairs. It tries to ensure that non-member states act according to its principles of international peace and security. UN members must offer every assistance in an approved UN action and in no way assist states against which the UN is taking preventive or enforcement action.

Today thousands of people visit the United Nations headquarters in New York city. They see the large rooms where representatives from more than 100 nations meet to discuss their problems. People who work for the United Nations believe that happy, healthy people are more likely to be friendly to other nations. They believe that helping people will help keep the world at peace.

Reading Comprehension from PRETCO

Task 1

Directions: *The following is part of a list from a book on WTO. After reading it, you are required to find the items equivalent to (与……相同的) those given in Chinese in the table below. Then you should put the corresponding letters in brackets numbered 1 to 5. (2005. 12)*

A—Dispute Settlement Body   B—Balance of International Payments

C—World Trade Organization   D—Risk Management

E— Investment in Non-productive Projects F—Grant the National Treatment to

G—Appeal Body   H—Common Agricultural Policy

I—Customs Value   J—Export Performance

K—Food Security　　　　　　L—Free Rider Problem

M—Grey Area Measures　　　　N—Import License

O—Market Access　　　　　　P—Marketing Board

Q—Presence of National Person　R—North American Free Trade Area

S—International Settlement　　　T—Peace Clause

U—Least-developed Countries　　V—Most-favored-nation Treatment

Example: (F) 实行国民待遇　　　　(P) 营销机构

1) (　　　　) 上诉机构　　　　(　　　　) 最惠国待遇

2) (　　　　) 和平条款　　　　(　　　　) 进口许可

3) (　　　　) 市场准入　　　　(　　　　) 非生产性投资

4) (　　　　) 食品安全　　　　(　　　　) 共同农业政策

5) (　　　　) 风险管理　　　　(　　　　) 争议处理机构

Task 2

Directions: *The following is part of a list from a book on WTO. After reading it, you are required to find the items equivalent to (与……相同的) those given in Chinese in the table below. Then you should put the corresponding letters in the brackets numbered 1 through 5. (2004. 06)*

A—World Trade Organization　　　B—Uruguay Round

C—Dispute Settlement Body　　　D—North American Free Trade Agreement

E—Common Market for Eastern and Southern Africa　F—Investment in Non-productive Projects

G—Risk Management　　　　　　H—Balance of International Payments

I—Appeal Body　　　　　　　　J—Bound Level

K—Common Agricultural Policy　　L—Customs Value

M—Environmentally Sound Technologies　N—Export Performance

O—Food Security　　　　　　　P—Trade Fair

Q—Technical Know-how Transfer　　R—North American Free Trade Area

S—Least-developed Countries　　　T—Intellectual Property Rights

U—Market Access　　　　　　　V—National Treatment

Example: (B) 乌拉圭回合 (J) 约束水平

1) ( ) 风险管理	( ) 最不发达国家
2) ( ) 市场准入	( ) 共同农业政策
3) ( ) 技术转让	( ) 非生产性投资
4) ( ) 上诉机构	( ) 北美自由贸易区
5) ( ) 知识产权	( ) 争议处理机构

Reading for Fun

Danish Air Force Compensates Santa

The Danish Air Force said it paid 31,175 kroner ($5,032) in compensation to a part-time Santa Claus whose reindeer died of heart failure when two fighter jets roared over his farm. The animal, named Rudolf, was grazing peacefully at the farm of Olavi Nikkanoff, when the screaming F-16 jets passed overhead at low altitude in this February. The reindeer collapsed and died, leaving Nikkanoff with the prospect of only one animal pulling his sleigh next Christmas.

He complained to the air force, which agreed to compensate him for the cost of the reindeer and veterinary expenses. "We got a letter from Santa complaining about his reindeer's death and looked into it seriously," said air force spokesman, Capt. Morten Jensen.

The air force checked flight data and veterinary reports and concluded the planes likely caused the animal's death. "We're more than happy to pay if it means that children around the world will get their presents," Jensen said. Nikkanoff said he was satisfied with the compensation and would use it to buy a new reindeer before Christmas.

Unit 4
Famous Celebrities

Passage A   Forever Anita Mui

Anita is the Cinderella of Hong Kong show business. She is also a legend in her time. In a short span of two to three years, she has risen from obscurity to become a superstar. She has been given various names and called almost everything, from praise like "The Madonna of the East" to abuse like "Cheap Slut". Why is this? What is it that arouses such violent and different responses?

Anita was born into a poor family. She had a job even when she was still studying. Life was never easy for her. Teamed with her sister, she plunged into the entertainment business at the age of five, when she had a contract to work at Lai Chi Kok Amusement Park. She did not make a name for herself but she got a lot of important training and experience.

Anita was never encouraged to read much. It was the radio and records that mainly influenced Anita. Music was the stabilizing influence in her life. The more she drew away from her family, the more she clung to music.

In those days Taiwan songs were popular. Anita heard the legendary Yiu So Yung (a Taiwan vocalist) and was so excited by her singing that she bought all her records—even though she couldn't really afford to. This is how Anita learnt her art from listening to records and the radio. A few years later, the Cantonese A-go-go caught on. Anita and her sister loved this A-go-go and learnt to perform it well. They were nicknamed "the Little Sorceresses" and were engaged by nightclubs. They did not attract the attention of serious record companies however.

In 1981 when she was seventeen, Anita won first place in the First New Talent Singing Awards Competition. Already quite a veteran of the nightclub stage, she was now about to become a working-class heroine. Winning the talent competition proved to be her first real step up the ladder of success. Capital Artists immediately saw Anita's potential and talked her into a long-term contract. From then on her fortune was made.

Eddie Lau the designer and image-maker and Michael Lai the musical producer of Capital Artists undertook to transform Anita. "Her showmanship is wonderful," said Eddie, "but we had to do something with her image. The gold dress she wore for the contest was so old-fashioned." Eddie got Anita to try out a number of costumes and finally decided on the new image. This proved to be a major breakthrough.

Instead of the shy, innocent look she had started out with, Anita now adopted the style of a bad girl. The change was powerful and proved a great success. Michael described Anita as one hell of a character behind a great voice and beautiful eyes.

Eddie and Michael collaborated closely in creating the new artist and matching songs with the image. The image developed the songs and the songs projected the image. Anita was always given a choice but she was easy-going and usually went along with their ideas. They found her eager to please and very cooperative. She even had her teeth straightened and was said to have undergone plastic surgery for her nose.

Eddie and Michael continued to make alterations to her image from album to album so that at every opportunity Anita had a fresh look and her excitement for the audience did not fade.

In early September 2003, Anita made the public announcement that she had cervical cancer to the media. Knowing that she would not make it past the illness, she had a final series of shows entitled the "Anita Classic Moments Live Concert". Anita eventually lost her battle to cervical cancer and died of respiratory complications leading to a lung failure at Hong Kong Sanatorium and Hospital on 30 December 2003. She was 40 years old. Thousands of fans turned out for her funeral in North Point in January 2004.

Ⓝew Words

1. adopt	*v.*	采用，使用
2. alteration	*n.*	变动，改动
3. award	*n.*	奖，奖赏，奖品
4. cling	*v.*	坚持，忠于
5. collaborate	*v.*	合作，协作
6. contract	*n.*	合同
7. cooperative	*a.*	合作的，协作的
8. costume	*n.*	服装
9. engage	*v.*	聘用某人，雇用某人
10. entertainment	*n.*	娱乐，文娱
11. entitle	*v.*	给……题名或命名
12. eventually	*ad.*	最后，最终
13. fade	*v.*	逐渐消失
14. image-maker	*n.*	形象顾问
15. innocent	*a.*	天真的，单纯的
16. legendary	*a.*	非常有名的，大名鼎鼎的

17. mandarin	*n.*	普通话
18. obscurity	*n.*	无名的人
19. potential	*n.*	潜力
20. project	*v.*	表明……的特点，使……的特点呈现
21. showmanship	*n.*	吸引观众的技巧
22. stabilising	*a.*	稳定的，安定的
23. straighten	*v.*	（使）弄直
24. transform	*v.*	改变，改造
25. veteran	*n.*	富有经验的人
26. vocalist	*n.*	歌手

Notes

1. She has been given various names and called almost everything, from praise like "The Madonna of the East" to abuse like "Cheap Slut".

   她曾经获得过各种各样的称呼，从称赞她为"东方的麦当娜"到谩骂她为"贱妇"，几乎什么都有。

2. Teamed with her sister, she plunged into the entertainment business at the age of five, when she had a contract to work at Lai Chi Kok Amusement Park.

   五岁的时候，她就与荔园游乐场签订了合同，与姐姐一起投身于娱乐行业。

   plunge into sth.: 开始从事，投身，例如，At the age of 52, he plunged into writing the first book or crime.

   Lai Chi Kok Amusement Park: 荔园游乐场，香港著名的游乐场。

3. Anita heard the legendary Yiu So Yung (a Taiwanese vocalist) and was so excited by her singing that she bought all her records—even though she couldn't really afford to.

   梅艳芳听到大名鼎鼎的的台湾歌手姚苏蓉的歌声后非常兴奋，于是把她所有的唱片都买了下来——尽管她当时并不是真的能买得起。

4. A few years later, the Cantonese A-go-go caught on. Anita and her sister loved this A-go-go and learnt to perform it well. They were nicknamed "the Little Sorceresses" and were engaged by nightclubs.

   几年以后，广东跳劲舞的娱乐活动流行起来。梅艳芳和她姐姐都很喜欢这种娱乐形式，她们把舞练得很好。由于表演非常精彩，她们被昵称为"小女巫"，并被夜总会聘用。

   catch on: 流行，风行，例如，It was a popular style in Britain but it never really caught on in America.

   nickname: 给某人起绰号，例如，He was nicknamed "smiler" because he was always cheerful.

Exercises

1. Choose the best answer.

1) Why does the author call Anita "the Cinderella of Hong Kong show business"?

   A. Because she is the princess of Hong Kong show business.

   B. Because she has risen from nobody to become a superstar.

   C. Because she has been given various names.

   D. Because she is very famous in Hong Kong show business.

2) Which of the following is NOT mentioned in the passage?

   A. Anita was born into a poor family.

   B. Anita had a happy childhood.

   C. Lai Chi Kok Amusement Park made a contract with Anita.

   D. Anita's family never encouraged Anita to read much.

3) Why did Capital Artists talk Anita into a long-term contract?

   A. Because she was quite a veteran of the nightclub stage.

   B. Because she was seventeen, old enough to sign a formal, long-term contract.

   C. Because she won first place in the competition and Capital Artists saw her potential.

   D. Because she was about to become a working-class heroine.

4) Who transformed Anita successfully?

   A. Capital Artists.

   B. Hong Kong entertainment circle.

   C. The Madonna of the East and the Cinderella of Hong Kong.

   D. Eddie Lau and Michael Lai.

5) Why did Anita change her image continuously?

   A. Because Eddie and Michael continued to make alterations to her image.

   B. Because Anita wanted to have a fresh look at every opportunity.

   C. Because Capital Artists asked her to do so.

   D. Because a fresh look would make her more attractive and popular and her excitement for the audience would not fade.

2. Complete the statements that follow the questions.

1) How was Anita's life when she was a child?

   Life was _____ for her.

2) What influenced Anita greatly?

   It was _____ that mainly influenced Anita.

3) How did Anita learn Yiu So Yung's art?

Anita learnt Yiu So Yung's art by _____.

4) What's Anita's original image?

Originally, she had _____.

5) How did Michael describe Anita?

Michael described Anita as _____ behind a great voice and beautiful eyes.

3. **Match the following words with the definitions below and then fill in the blanks with their proper forms.**

obscurity	arouse	violent	costume	cling
engage	veteran	potential	undergo	innocent
cooperative	collaborate	alteration	fade	transform

1) (*noun*) a change in the appearance or form of sth.

We are making a few _____ to the house.

2) (*noun*) a person with much or long experience, especially a soldier

The two old men standing before the window are _____ of the Second World War.

3) (*adjective*) knowing nothing of evil or wrong

I'm not quite so _____ as to believe that.

4) (*adjective*) willing to cooperate; helpful

All of us made _____ efforts to complete the assignment.

5) (*noun*) a state in which a person is not well known or not remembered

He was a famous poet, but he died in _____.

6) (*verb*) to arrange to employ sb.; hire sb.

We _____ him as technical adviser since no one could operate this machine.

7) (*noun*) a set of clothes that are typical of a particular place or historical period of time

The dancers were all in national _____.

8) (*verb*) to disappear gradually; vanish

All memory of the past has _____ with the time passing by.

9) (*noun*) the inherent ability or capacity to develop or achieve sth. in the future

We want each student to realize their full _____.

10) (*verb*) to make you become interested, expect sth.

The odd sight in the sky _____ our curiosity.

11) (*verb*) unwilling to abandon sth.; refuse to give sth. up

She _____ to the hope that he was still alive.

12) (*verb*) to work together, especially in a joint intellectual effort

Professor Smith decided to _____ on a book with his colleagues.

13) (*verb*) to completely change the appearance or character of sb. or sth.

She used to be terribly shy but a year abroad has completely _____ her.

14) (*verb*) to experience sth., especially sth. that is unpleasant but necessary

She _____ emergency surgery in hospital last month.

15) (*adjective*) showing or caused by very strong emotions

There was a very _____ reaction from the public.

Reading Skills

Ⓢkimming

略读

　　略读是指以一个人可能达到的最快速度浏览整篇文章。当读者的目的是了解文章主要思想时，略读是最有效的阅读方式，其特点是注重整体，忽略细节。有效的略读要处理好两个方面的问题，即文章的哪些部分应该详读，哪些部分应该略读。略读时，既求速度快，又要抓住重点。略读时应着重注意以下几个方面：

　　1. 文章的标题、副标题、开头和结尾。文章的标题是对文章内容的高度概括，副标题则是对标题的补充说明，因此略读时，要首先注意文章的标题和副标题。一般说来，作者常常在文章的开头介绍其将要探讨的问题，在文章结束时得出结论，因此，要特别关注文章的开头和结尾。

　　2. 每一段的主题句。主题句一般位于段落的首部或尾部，有时也会居于段落的中间，因此，要格外注意段落的首句和尾句。如果该段没有主题句，要通读全段，找出重要的句子，了解该段的中心思想。

3. 关键信号词。作者通常会用一些信号词或关联词来安排文章的篇章结构和轻重主次。根据这些信号词，我们能够快速确定阅读时应着重注意的部分，同时舍弃一些次要的细节。表示举例的信号词，例如for example/instance等，后面的内容不是要点，只是例子，可以跳过不读。而表示结论的信号词，如in conclusion，therefore等等，后面的内容一定要密切关注。还有一些罗列要点的信号词，如firstly, secondly, finally等，只看其后面的要点，忽略细节。

[例] Today, music takes many forms around the world. The music of people in Europe and America is known as Western music. There are two chief kinds of Western music, classical and popular. Classical music includes symphonies, operas, and ballets. Popular music includes country music, folk music, jazz, and rock music. The cultures of Africa and Asia have developed their own types of classical and popular music.

What is the main idea of the passage?

A. Western music includes two chief kinds: classical and popular.

B. Music takes many forms all over the world nowadays.

C. The music of people in Europe and America is known as Western music.

D. The cultures of Africa and Asia have developed their own types of music.

问题是要求找出本段的主旨大意。通过快速浏览本段的首句和尾句，我们可以看出段首句是主题句，因此，这个问题在第一句中就可以找到答案——Today, music takes many forms around the world. 通过略读，我们很快得知正确答案是B选项。

[例] "But I just paid $1.69 for this bottle of wine last week. How come the price is now $2.25? what's going on?"

There are at least three things going on that have caused the price of wine to rise. All have to do with the supply and demand factors of economics.

The first factor is that people drink more wine than ever before. This demand for more wine has increased overall wine sales in America at the rate of 15 percent a year.

The second factor is that the supply of wine has stayed relatively the same, which means that the same number of bottles is produced each year. Wine producers are trying to open up new land to grow more grapes. But in at least three wine-producing areas of the world—France, Germany and California—new vineyards will not be available in the near future. Wines are produced in other countries, such as Italy, Spain and Australia, but none of these countries will be able to fill the demand for good wines.

The third factor is that costs of wine productions are increasing. The men who make wine are asking for more money, and the machinery needed to press the grapes is becoming more expensive.

When the demand for something is greater than the supply, prices go up. When production costs, meaning the prices of labor and machinery rise, the producer adds this increase to the price of the wine.

1) From the first paragraph, we know that the speaker is _____.
   A. asking about the price   B. worrying about the price
   C. bargaining over the price   D. complaining about the price

2) The three factors mentioned in the passage cause _____.
   A. the sales of wine to increase   B. the price of wine to go up
   C. the production of wine to decrease   D. more and more people to drink wine

3) What does "production costs" refer to in the last paragraph?
   A. The price of grapes and machines.
   B. The cost of land and transportation.
   C. The price of wine and wine bottles.
   D. The cost of manpower and equipment.

4) The author's purpose of writing this passage is to _____.
   A. persuade people to drink less wine
   B. tell people where to get the best wine
   C. explain why the price of wine is rising
   D. show that wine is popular with Americans

本文主要分析了葡萄酒价格上涨的三个原因，都和经济学的供求关系有关。文章后面设置的四个问题，用略读的方法，在文章中都能找到答案。

问题1：From the first paragraph, we know that the speaker is _____.

略读第一段，只要理解 "What's going on?" 是带有怨气地质问价格为何上涨，就能选出正确答案D。

问题2：The three factors mentioned in the passage cause _____.

第二段第一句话即阐述了三个因素造成的后果——价格上涨（B）。后面几小节都是具体说明三个因素的内容，所以可以忽略不看。

问题3：What does "production costs" refer to in the last paragraph?

根据问题，只要略读最后一段，找到关键词production costs即可选出正确答案D。

问题4：The author's purpose of writing this passage is to _____.

通过略读得知：第一段说话人抱怨价格上涨；第二段总述上涨的三个原因；第三、四、五段具体分析三个原因；第六段总结说明供求关系、生产成本和价格的关系。全文都在分析葡萄酒价格上涨问题，所以C为正确答案。

Exercises

1. Skim the following passage and choose the best answer.

In July, 2001, swimmer Zhang Jian became the first Chinese person who swam across the English Channel as he successfully landed in Calais, France, after a 12-hour journey from Dover, Britain. The 33.8-kilometre channel has attracted many adventure-seekers because it is one of the most difficult to cross.

The 37-year-old swimmer left Shakespeare Beach, Dover, to start his feat. He was guided in the effort by a pilot ship. With special oil on his skin to help keep warm, Zhang Jian beat the cold currents of 16℃ and swam for 12 hours. At first, Zhang swam freestyle to save energy. Then he altered his style along the way because the ocean currents changed every six hours and the water was so cold. Zhang switched over to the breaststroke during his swimming, although experts warned that doing so would exhaust him faster. Later he changed back to freestyle. Zhang kept up with the rising tide, helping himself achieve the goal.

Most Chinese news Websites covered Zhang's exploits extensively. "The spirit of adventure which has long been far away from Chinese should come back to us", said an Internet user. "Whether he succeeds or fails, he has given us something quite valuable", said another online message.

1) Why has the English Channel attracted many adventure-seekers?
   A. Because it is the most difficult channel to cross.
   B. Because it is 33.8-kilometre long.
   C. Because it is one of the most difficult channels to cross.
   D. Because Zhang Jian swam across it successfully.

2) What kind of swimming style will make Zhang's energy give out faster?
   A. Freestyle.   B. Breaststroke.
   C. Backstroke.   D. Butterfly.

3) Which of the following statements is TRUE?
   A. At first Zhang swam breaststroke to save energy.
   B. The ocean currents changed irregularly, so Zhang altered his style along the way.
   C. Zhang didn't follow the experts' advice in the beginning.
   D. Freestyle is a kind of swimming style which can easily make people exhausted.

4) What does the sentence "The spirit of adventure which has long been far away from Chinese should come back to us" mean?
   A. We should seek adventure in the English Channel although it is far away from China.
   B. More Chinese should attempt to cross the English Channel with the spirit of adventure.
   C. The spirit of adventure is buried beneath the busyness of modern life.

D. The positive spirit of adventure which was once lost should be promoted.

5) Which of the following would be the best title for the passage?

A. How to Cross the English Channel

B. Courage Conquers All

C. Chinese Swimmer Crossed the English Channel

D. Zhang Jian's Exploits

Passage B Ted Turner—the Founder of CNN

Read the passage and judge whether the following statements are true (T) or false (F).

1) According to the passage, Turner is not only the founder of CNN but also a philanthropist.

2) The broadcasting company he had built from scratch went bankrupt in spring 2000.

3) Turner's marriage ended in divorce because his wife Jane became a born-again Christian.

4) Two of Turner's grandchildren gained a rare genetic disease.

5) Turner's UN Foundation helped women from Vietnam start businesses selling nut butter.

6) Nigel Pritchard has prepared a memo outlining things his boss might avoid talking about.

7) Turner is infamous for doing as he pleases.

8) Turner sees himself as engaged in a personal battle against apocalypse.

9) Turner had a happy and carefree childhood.

10) Turner's father believed that instilling insecurity in his son would help him to achieve success.

Turner is the 63-year-old multibillionaire founder of CNN, former champion sailor, Rhett Butler lookalike and record-breaking philanthropist.

Turner has just emerged from the worst two years of his life—years that he has said left him feeling "suicidal". In spring 2000, he was suddenly sidelined from the broadcasting company he had built from scratch. Then his wife of eight years, the actress Jane Fonda, came home one night and informed him that she was now a born-again Christian; they divorced last year. Two of his grandchildren developed a rare genetic disorder, and one died. Turner's friends said he was inconsolable (极为伤心的). Then, just when he felt it could get no worse, he brought the wrath of America upon himself by a speech in Rhode Island saying that the September 11 hijackers (劫机犯)

had been "brave".

Then he threw himself into his charity work. Turner's UN Foundation, the biggest of his three charities, recently spent $22.2 million in one month combating intestinal parasites in Vietnamese children, reducing China's greenhouse-gas emissions and helping women from Burkina Faso start businesses selling nut butter.

Nigel Pritchard, CNN's head of international public relations, who is sitting beside me,

Newspapers gone in a decade

CKLN to use antenna thanks to the CBC

Ted Turner, owner of a 24-hour TV news station in the U.S., says Canadian laws are preventing us from witnessing "journalistic history."

has prepared a memo outlining some things his boss might like to consider not saying. It politely suggests that he might steer clear of talking about AOL Time Warner, and, specifically, he might like to avoid reference to that Rhode Island speech. Turner is notorious (声名狼藉的) for doing as he pleases. Early in his career, he made a pitch wearing no clothes to advertising executives; later, he went to Cuba (古巴) to get Fidel Castro (菲德尔·卡斯特罗) to tape a promotional slot for CNN.

He has various worldsaving projects: from preventing the extinction of the Chiricahua leopard frog (奇里卡瓦豹蛙) in the wilds of New Mexico to founding an influential nuclear non-proliferation institute. Turner really does seem to see himself as locked in a personal battle against apocalypse (大灾难). He doesn't just give money: his staff are sometimes taken aback to see him skulking in the streets nearby, picking up litter.

When Turner gave his first billion to the UN, he dropped 67 laces on the Forbes (福布斯) 500 rich list, out of the top 10 for ever. (His fortune now stands at $3.8 billion.)

It isn't hard to see how Turner's childhood might have instilled this sense of permanent crisis, of desperate insecurity, behind the frenzied activity that is his trademark. His father, from whom he inherited an advertising business that he turned into CNN, was prone to fits of rage, and beat him with a coat hanger; he committed suicide when Turner was 24. Even before that, his younger sister had died from an immune disease when she was 12, and Turner was sent to a boarding school he hated. His father, he has said, not without admiration, believed that instilling insecurity in his son would help him to achieve. All in all, Turner seems to have been a well-qualified candidate for total psychic collapse (精神崩溃). "But when everything goes wrong," he says today, "you can either give up or you can try to fight. I tried to fight."

Reading Comprehension from PRETCO

Task 1

Directions: *After reading the following passage, you will find 5 questions or unfinished statements. For each question or statement there are 4 choices marked A, B, C and D. You should make the correct choice and mark the corresponding letter with a single line through the center. (2006. 01)*

Most of us grow up taking certain things for granted. We tend to assume that experts and religious leaders tell us "the truth". We tend to believe that things advertised on television or in newspapers can't be bad for us.

However, encouragement of critical thinking in students is one of the goals of most colleges and universities. Few professors require students to share the professors' own beliefs. In general, professors are more concerned that students learn to question and critically examine the arguments of others, including some of their own beliefs or values. This does not mean that professors insist that you change your beliefs, either. It does mean, however, professors will usually ask you to support the views you express in class or in your writing.

If your premises (前提) are shaky, or if your arguments are not logical, professors personally point out the false reasoning in your arguments. Most professors want you to learn to recognize the premises of your arguments, to examine whether you really accept these premises, and to understand whether or not you draw logical conclusions. Put it in this way: Professors don't tell you what to think; they try to teach you how to think.

On the other hand, if you intend to disagree with your professors in class, you should be prepared to offer a strong argument in support of your ideas. Arguing just for the sake of arguing usually does not promote a critical examination of ideas. Many professors interpret it as rudeness.

1) In the first paragraph, the writer tries to tell us that people _____.
   A. easily accept certain things without a second thought
   B. grow up through learning certain things in life
   C. are forming their views during their growth
   D. have strong beliefs in authorities while getting old

2) Nowadays, most colleges and universities encourage students to _____.
   A. criticize others
   B. share professors' beliefs
   C. give their own ideas
   D. change their own beliefs

3) The word "shaky" (Line 1, Para. 3) most probably means "_____".
   A. creative   B. firm
   C. false   D. weak

4) To help students develop their critical thinking, professors mainly teach them _____.
   A. choice of their premises
   B. the way to think independently
   C. skills of drawing conclusions
   D. different kinds of argument

5) According to the writer, the right way to argue is to _____.
   A. argue mainly for the sake of arguing
   B. prove it with a good conclusion
   C. support your idea with sound reasoning
   D. examine others' ideas critically

Task 2

Directions: *This part is to test your reading ability. There are 5 questions or unfinished statements. For each question or statement there are 4 choices marked A, B, C and D. You should make the correct choice and mark the corresponding letter with a single line through the center. (2005. 01)*

The human body has developed its millions of nerves to be highly aware of what goes on both inside and outside of it. This helps us adjust to the outside world. Without our nerves and our brain, which is a system of nerves, we couldn't know what is happening. But we pay for our sensitivity. We can feel pain when the slightest thing is wrong with any part of our body. This history of torture (折磨) is based on the human body being open to pain.

But there is a way to handle pain. Look at the Indian fakir (苦行僧) who sits on a bed of nails. Fakirs can put a needle right through an arm, and feel no pain. This ability that some humans have developed to handle pain should give us ideas about how the mind can deal with pain.

The big thing in withstanding pain is our attitude towards it. If the dentist says, "This will hurt a little," it helps us to accept the pain. By staying relaxed, and by treating the pain as an interesting sensation (感觉), we can handle the pain without falling apart. After all, although pain is an unpleasant sensation, it is still a sensation, and sensations are the stuff of life.

1) The human body has developed a system of nerves that enables us to _____.
   A. stay relaxed   B. avoid pain   C. stand torture   D. feel pain

2) What does the writer mean by saying "we pay for our sensitivity" in the first paragraph?
   A. We have to take care of our sense of pain.

B. We suffer from our sense of feeling.

C. We should try hard to resist pain.

D. We are hurt when we feel pain.

3) When the author mentions the Indian fakir, he shows that _____.

A. fakirs possess magic power

B. Indians are not afraid of pain

C. people can learn to cope with pain

D. some people are born without a sense of pain

4) What is essential for people to stand pain according to the writer?

A. Their relaxation.   B. Their interest.

C. Their nerves.   D. Their attitude.

5) The author believes that _____.

A. feeling pain is part of our life

B. pain should be avoided at all cost

C. feeling pain can be an interesting thing

D. magic power is essential for reducing pain

Reading for Fun

A Hot Proposal

To prove his love, a 38-year-old man set himself on fire before getting down on one knee and asking his girlfriend to marry him. About 100 people gathered to watch Todd Grannis perform the flaming stunt, which involved wearing a cape soaked in gasoline. Grannis climbed up a 10-foot scaffold, was set on fire and then plunged into a swimming pool, dousing the blaze (把火弄灭).

Emerging unscathed, he got down on one knee and proposed, as a friend standing nearby slipped him the engagement ring. "Honey, you make me hot," he told his sweetheart, Malissa Kusiek. "I hope you'll understand that I'm on fire for you." Kusiek, who has been dating Grannis for several years, said "yes", but added that she was a little angry because of the danger. "At first I was mad, because I thought, 'He's not a stuntman,'" Kusiek said. "Then, of course, the tears started flowing. Of course I said yes. I was so thrilled." Grannis said he came up with the stunt through the help of his friend, professional stuntman Eric Barkey. Barkey pulled out a photo of himself on fire and said, "You could do that," Grannis said. Grannis met Kusiek, the owner of a local hair salon, when she cut his hair.

Unit 5
Living with Mobiles

Passage A Can We Live Without Our Mobile Phones?

My name is Damian and I'm a mobile-phone addict. I am here today to face the truth about my condition and hope that by speaking out I can help others to overcome their own problems.

The casual observer probably couldn't detect anything wrong with me. I have a respectable appearance and my behavior in public isn't shocking or conspicuous. I hadn't even realised myself that I was a mobile phonoholic, until the past few days. But I have just spent two of those days conducting an experiment that has revealed the awful reality: I have suffered mentally and physically. And my experience has convinced me that I am only one of millions of fellow addicts. You may well be one yourself.

I have just attempted to live my life without a mobile phone.

Mobile phones have been the biggest agent of change in the daily behavior of Britons in the past decade. Today there are more than 55 million mobile phone subscribers in Britain, a huge leap from less than 10 million users in 1997. As the size of the handsets has diminished, their influence has grown, altering the speed and frequency of our communication with each other, quickening the pace of decision-making and altering radically the way we plan our working and social lives.

Switching it off at the beginning of Day 1 was strange. For the past few years I have done this only when boarding an aircraft. Even on holiday—and this may strike you as rather sad—I put the phone in silent mode and annoy my wife by checking it at least every few hours.

I should have left the phone at home, or at least put it in a drawer for two days. But I couldn't bring myself to do that, so I left it sitting on my desk. For the first few hours of abstinence I kept involuntarily picking it up and looking at the display to see if I had any messages or had missed a call, only to see that it was, of course, switched off.

When I had got used to the fact that it was off, I still picked it up, turned it over in my hand and fiddled with it, like a smoker fidgeting with a packet of cigarettes. I realised that I had a whole routine of nervous tics involving my phone and that these were exacerbated by my desire to use it. I took these to be the physical effects of undergoing the process of withdrawal.

These two days were mostly office-bound and I didn't need to use my phone to do my job. I can't imagine how I would have been able to operate if I had been out on a story. Like anyone working on the hoof away from the office the phone is glued to my ear and I can make and receive dozens of calls a day.

When I switched the phone back on after two days I had three messages and four texts. OK, so I was a bit put out that there were not more. I had missed the chance to do a phone interview that I had been trying to secure for two weeks and an invitation to a last-minute lunch. Frustrating, but to be honest, no more than that.

I remain convinced that the phone is a cruical tool for work, but realise that otherwise it is often just a pointless security blanket: "Hi, darling. I'm on my way home. Just leaving the office now. Love you. Byeeee."

New Words

1. abstinence	*n.*	节制	
2. addict	*n.*	入迷的人，有瘾的人	
3. awful	*a.*	可怕的，糟糕的	
4. alter	*v.*	改变	
5. blanket	*n.*	毯子	
6. board	*v.*	上（船、飞机等）	
7. casual	*a.*	不经意的，不关心的	
8. conspicuous	*a.*	惹人注意的	
9. crucial	*a.*	至关紧要的	
10. diminish	*v.*	（使）减少，（使）缩小	
11. exacerbate	*v.*	使加剧	
12. fiddle	*v.*	（尤指厌烦或紧张地）不断摆弄	
13. frustrating	*a.*	令人沮丧的	
14. glue	*v.*	胶合，粘贴	
15. hoof	*n.*	蹄	
16. involuntarily	*ad.*	不知不觉地，无心地	
17. phonoholic	*n.*	手机迷	
18. radically	*ad.*	完全地，彻底地	
19. reveal	*v.*	显示，揭示，暴露	
20. routine	*n.*	惯例，常规	
21. secure	*v.*	获得，得到	

22. subscriber	n.	用户
23. switch	v.	（用开关）转换，切换
24. tic	n.	无意识的习惯行为
25. withdrawal	n.	脱瘾过程

Notes

1. I have a respectable appearance and my behavior in public isn't shocking or conspicuous.

   我外表体面，在公共场合的行为也算中规中矩。

   respectable: （行为，外观等）体面得体的，例如，Let's make you look a bit more respectable before you go out.

   shocking: 令人气愤的，令人厌恶的，例如，What she did was so shocking that I can hardly describe it.

2. I hadn't even realised myself that I was a mobile phonoholic, until the past few days.

   直到最近几天我才意识到自己是个手机迷。

   mobile phonoholic: 手机迷，-oholic和-aholic是后缀，解释为"……迷，……狂"，例如，workaholic，工作狂，alcoholic，酗酒者

3. I realised that I had a whole routine of nervous tics involving my phone and that these were exacerbated by my desire to use it.

   我意识到我已经形成了一连串不自觉的习惯性行为，并且想用手机的强烈欲望加剧了这种行为。

4. These two days were mostly office-bound and I didn't need to use my phone to do my job.

   这两天大多数时间都是在办公室里待着，因此不需要用手机来完成工作。

   -bound: 后缀，表示"受限于……的，不能离开……"，例如，office-bound，整日呆在办公室里的，类似的还有desk-bound, bed-bound等。

5. I can't imagine how I would have been able to operate if I had been out on a story.

   我简直无法想象，如果在外采访没有手机的话，我该怎么办？

   out on a story: 在外采访以撰写新闻报道

6. Like anyone working on the hoof away from the office the phone is glued to my ear and I can make and receive dozens of calls a day.

   和任何一个在外办公的人一样，我把手机耳机线一直戴在耳朵上，一天要接几十个电话。

   on the hoof: 在做某事时（尤指在去某地的途中），例如，We can grab some lunch on the hoof.

7. OK, so I was a bit put out that there were not more.

没有更多的电话和短信，为此我有些恼火。

be/feel put out: 感到烦乱，恼火，例如，We are a little put out at not being invited to the wedding.

8. I remain convinced that the phone is a crucial tool for work, but realise that otherwise it is often just a pointless security blanket.

我仍然相信手机对于工作来说非常重要，但我也意识到除了有利于工作外，手机对我们来说常常像是把毫无意义的保护伞。

a pointless security blanket: 无意义的保护伞。security blanket这个习语的流行是由于报上连载的一部幽默连环画里的主人公。美国人都爱看这连环画，尤其喜欢其中的主人公小男孩。他从早到晚都带着夜里睡觉盖的毯子，因为他只要一坐到地板上吮吸大拇指或者那条毯子的一角，心里就踏实，觉得特别有安全感。于是人们就把带给人安全感的人或者事物称为security blanket。

Ⓔxercises

1. Choose the best answer.

1) How many days did the author spend conducting an experiment on living his life without a mobile phone?

A. Two days.　　　B. Three days.　　　C. Four days.　　　D. Five days.

2) According to the author, how many mobile phone subscribers are there in Britain nowadays?

A. Less than 10 million.

B. Less than 20 million.

C. More than 55 million.

D. Not given in the passage.

3) In what occasion would the author switch his mobile phone off?

A. On holiday.

B. When boarding an aircraft.

C. On weekends.

D. Off duty.

4) Which of the following statements is TRUE according to the passage?

A. The author left his mobile phone at home for two days.

B. The author left his mobile phone in a drawer for two days.

C. For the first few hours of abstinence the author kept involuntarily picking his mobile phone up and looking at the display.

D. When the author got used to the fact that his mobile phone was off, he stopped fiddling with it.

5) "Hi, darling. I'm on my way home. Just leaving the office now. Love you. Byeeee." This example in the last paragraph is to illustrate that _____.

   A. the mobile phone is often just a pointless security blanket

   B. the mobile phone is a cruical tool for work

   C. the author decided to stop using the mobile phone

   D. the coverage of mobile phones has extended

2. Complete the statements that follow the questions.

1) What did the author hope by speaking out the truth about his condition?

   He hoped that he could help others to _____.

2) Why couldn't the casual observer detect anything wrong with the author?

   Because he has _____ and his behavior in public isn't shocking or conspicuous.

3) What has been the biggest agent of change in the daily behavior of Britons in the past decade?

   _____.

4) What did the author do when he had got used to the fact that his mobile phone was off?

   He still picked it up, turned it over in his hand and _____ it.

5) What can you learn after reading the text?

   We can learn from the text that mobile phones have already _____ on people's lives.

3. Match the following words with the definitions below and then fill in the blanks with their proper forms.

alter	addict	diminish	fiddle	crucial
conspicuous	reveal	respectable	casual	secure
awful	fellow	withdrawal	frustrating	routine

1) (*noun*) someone who is addicted

   We shouldn't ignore the fact that many middle school students are video game _____.

2) (*verb*) to touch or move sth. with many small quick movements of your fingers because you are bored, nervous, or concentrating on sth. else

   She _____ with the sugar packet, avoiding his eyes.

3) (*adjective*) very noticeable or easy to see, especially because of being unusual or different

She's always _____ because of her bright clothes and queer hair style.

4) (*verb*) to change or make sb. or sth. change

These clothes are too large; they must be _____.

5) (*verb*) to make known sth. that was previously secret or unknown

Neither side _____ what was discussed at the meeting.

6) (*adjective*) not showing much care or thought

It was just a _____ remark—I wasn't really serious.

7) (*noun*) the usual or normal way in which you do things

I arrive at nine o'clock, teach until twelve thirty and then have a meal; that is my morning _____.

8) (*adjective*) making you feel annoyed, upset, or impatient because you cannot do what you want to do

After three hours' _____ delay, the train at last arrived.

9) (*noun*) a retreat or retirement

Our chief representative's _____ could be considered as a protest.

10) (*verb*) to get or achieve sth. important, especially after a lot of effort

UN negotiators are still trying to _____ the release of the hostages.

11) (*adjective*) used for talking about people who are similar to you or in the same situation as you

Discuss your experiences with a _____ student.

12) (*adjective*) obeying the moral or social standards that are accepted by most people

He makes his living in a perfectly _____ trade.

13) (*adjective*) extremely significant or important

Winning this contract is _____ to the success of the company.

14) (*adjective*) extremely bad or unpleasant

The first half of the year 2008 was _____. A big snowstorm was closely followed by a terrible earthquake.

15) (*verb*) to make sth. smaller or less

It is not impossible that human beings will live on nothing because the world's resources are rapidly _____.

Reading Skills

Ⓓetailed Reading
细读

细读（detailed-reading）指在对全文有整体印象的前提下进行的深入细致的阅读。细读的要求是了解各段主要意思和文章细节，并在此基础上进行推断。在做阅读理解题时，除了首先要抓住文章的主旨和大意外，还必须弄清楚文中的一些重要细节或事实。和细读相关的题目称为细节题。细节题在阅读理解中占相当大的比重，涉及的内容很广，如时间、地点、人物、数字、原因、结果、文字结构等。细节题的常见提问形式有：

1. According to the passage, when/where/what/who/how/why...?
2. Which of the following statements is (NOT) TRUE?
3. What is the meaning of the word "..." in Line X, Para. X ?
4. The word "..." in Line X, Para. X can be replaced by...?
5. Which of the following statements is not mentioned in the passage?
6. The fact/evidence, etc. that the author bases the statements on is...?

这些细节题的设置细化到了文章中某一要点，某一句话。提问的出发点基于文章中的具体阐述。所以，解答这类题目时，不要偏离原文，而要针对题目的内容，到文章中有的放矢地去细读，去寻找相关的信息，然后仔细推敲，得出正确答案。

[例] We have everything college students need to know about GM's Cooperative Education and Intern Programs in our Student Center. Each fall, GM recruiters (招聘人员) visit the campuses of many of the nation's top engineering and business colleges and universities to recruit students. These students are considered for interesting assignments throughout our US operations. Check out our Recruiting Calendar to see if GM will be visiting your campus. If your campus is not listed, please apply online.

Will GM start your career moving? Fasten your seat belt!

For full-time college students, General Motors offers both a Cooperative Education and an Intern Program. Participants in these real-business-world educational programs gain valuable degree-related experience, develop an insider's understanding of how GM works and earn competitive wages. These programs are designed to provide GM with a source of highly talented candidates while giving students an opportunity for hands-on experience in their chosen field. As a result, participants in these programs are given serious consideration for full-time positions with GM when they graduate. Candidates for these programs must successfully complete an online assessment and possess qualifications that match the business needs of the organization.

   1) GM is likely to recruit college students for its programs who _____.
     A. do a full-time college program
     B. major in engineering and business

C. have had some practical experience

D. have gathered information about GM

2) The Recruiting Calendar (Line 5, Para. 1) gives the information about _____.

A. the kinds of people GM needs to train

B. the nation's top colleges and universities

C. GM recruiters' visits to colleges and universities

D. The interesting tasks GM expects the students to fulfill

3) Those students whose university is not listed on the Recruiting Calendar may _____.

A. apply to GM online

B. be given interesting tasks

C. come to the GM's training offices directly

D. invite recruiters to visit their universities

4) The programs that GM offers to full-time college students will help them to _____.

A. gain information about business in general

B. get business experience and good wages

C. develop their talents fully

D. obtain a higher degree

5) GM offers the Cooperative Education and Intern Programs in order to _____.

A. make its business needs known to the public

B. perform successful online assessments

C. advertise its newly-designed products

D. find out highly talented candidates

这篇文章的大意是：学生中心为大学生提供有关通用汽车公司合作教育项目以及实习项目的一切信息。通用公司通常在秋季招聘大学生。要了解有关信息，可以查阅通用公司的招聘日程表。如果你的学校没有列入表内，你可以网上申请。通用的这些项目可以给学生许多帮助，等等。文章后面设置了五个问题。这五个问题全都是细节题。答题时，需要把文章细细阅读，找出相关答案。

问题1：GM is likely to recruit college students for its programs who _____.

细读文章第一段得知，通用公司每年会去美国顶尖的工学院和商学院招聘大学生，因此正确答案应是B。

问题2：The Recruiting Calendar (Line 5, Para. 1) gives the information about _____.

文章第一段第四句话告诉我们，想要了解通用的招聘人员会不会去贵校，可以查阅通用的招聘日程表。由此可知，招聘日程表提供了招聘人员要去的学校。因此，该题应选C。

问题3：Those students whose university is not listed on the Recruiting Calendar may _____.

这一细节同样在第一段中可以找到答案。本段最后一句告诉我们，如果你的学校没有列入表内，可以在网上申请。因此正确答案是A。

问题4：The programs that GM offers to full-time college students will help them to _____.

文章第三段第二句告诉我们：学生可以获得宝贵经验，深入了解通用的运作模式，获取丰厚的薪水。在四个选项中，B符合上述内容，所以是正确答案。

问题5：GM offers the Cooperative Education and Intern Programs in order to _____.

文章第三段第三句话告诉我们：这些项目的目的在于给通用培养优秀人才并为大学生提供机会。虽然选项D没有完全复述原文，但内容相似，只是换了一种表述方式，因此D为正确答案。

Exercises

Read the following paragraph and choose the best answer.

Melbourne, with a population of over 3.5 million, is the second largest city in Australia. It is clean, safe, dynamic and exciting, and well-known internationally for its universities and other educational institutions. The city has well-planned tree-lined wide streets and many beautiful parks and gardens. It has a good transport system of roads, buses, trains, and trams (电车). The La Trobe University (拉特罗布大学) campus is connected to the Central Business District by trams, express buses, and bus and train connections. Melbourne is a culturally rich city, and is home to large communities of people from all parts of Europe, the Americas, Africa, and Asia. The city is famous for its restaurant, theatres, music, opera, ballet, art, culture, and shops, and a lively and dynamic nightlife. Melbourne people are enthusiastic about sports, and the city hosts many famous international sports events. Near Melbourne there are beautiful coastlines with excellent beaches, national parks, forests, wineries (葡萄酒厂), winter snowfields and summer resorts. The climate is temperate and comfortable, with warm summers and cool winters. In summer, maximum daytime temperatures range from 26℃ to 36℃, and in winter from 12℃ to 18℃. The weather in Melbourne can be variable from day to day. In 2002, Melbourne was rated the world's best city to live in by the Economist Intelligence Unit.

1) Melbourne is well-known in the world for its _____.
   A. large population   B. educational institutions
   C. transport system   D. beautiful parks and gardens

2) According to the passage, Melbourne is a city where _____.
   A. rich people choose to live   B. the best wine is produced
   C. various cultures exist   D. Asian food is popular

3) Melbourne people are very interested in _____.

   A. sports   B. sunbathing   C. sightseeing   D. traveling

4) The word "temperate" in the sentence "The climate is temperate" (Line 12), most probably means _____.

   A. hot   B. mild   C. dry   D. cold

5) The best title for the passage might be _____.

   A. An Ideal Place for Shopping

   B. A City with the Best Climate

   C. The World's Best City to Live In

   D. The World's Most Beautiful City

Passage B   Mobile Phones

Read the passage and judge whether the following statements are true (T) or false (F).

1) When the bank clerk found out the author didn't have a mobile phone, she simply thought the author was very poor.

2) The author refused all the modern electrical appliances or digital products.

3) It never occurred to the author to get a mobile phone.

4) The guy who had a parachuting accident didn't have his mobile phone with him.

5) Mobile phones could be useful if there was a real emergency. But that's not always the case.

6) Three men died in the awful story of the Kenyan student because they were so desperate for the money.

7) The bright light from the mobile phone used in the cinema annoyed the author.

8) A mobile phone can be used to give an excuse for being late.

9) The advantages of the mobile phone outweigh its disadvantages according to the author.

10) The author felt that the mobile phone was a real nuisance rather than convenience.

I don't have one, and if I can help it, I won't ever get one in the future. And I hate the assumption that I need one, or that I'm strange for not having one. I opened a new bank account the other day and the woman who was helping me asked me if I was serious when she found out I didn't have one.

She simply couldn't see how I could live my life without one. I don't see why—I can be contacted at home, or work, so what's the problem?

Yes, I have a laptop computer and instant access to the Internet; yes, I have a digital camera and yes I have a microwave oven and an i-Pod but I absolutely refuse to get a mobile phone!

Of course I can see how useful they could be, and that if there was a real emergency they could come in handy, but that's not always the case. There was a story of a guy who had a parachuting accident and found himself on top of a cliff with two broken legs. He had his mobile with him but—guess what? He wasn't able to use it because he was in

a remote area! So, in great pain, he had to pull himself along the ground with his elbows until he got to a road and could stop a motorist. So not much help for him then, was it?

Other times they create the emergency themselves. Remember that awful story of the Kenyan student? She dropped hers into a pit latrine while "answering a call of nature". So she offered the equivalent of $13 to anyone who could get it for her and what happened? Three men died, intoxicated (使中毒) by the fumes because they were so desperate for the money. That's awful.

But these aren't my main bugbears. No, what I hate is how my daily life is affected negatively by other people using theirs. Take a restaurant for example. I really, really hate it when friends arrive and the first thing they do is put their mobiles on the table so that, in the event of it going off they stop talking to you and start ignoring you. Are they doctors? Are they giving advice on open-heart surgery? Are they talking to long-lost friends? Sick relatives? No! It'll be their mother who they saw recently, or other friends they're going to meet soon. For me it's rudeness. And of course I also have to put up with the same happening on the next-door table too. And how inept (不适当的) and pointless the conversations! "I'm with Jenny and we're having Dim Sum." The person needs to know that? "Hi, I'm on the train now and will be there in about 10 minutes." So? Are they not expected? Can't they just turn up in 10 minutes and say "I'm here"?

I'm also affected by the light—do the owners really not realize how bright they are? OK, maybe the stupid thing is on vibration (振动) but when it's opened in the cinema, or at a concert the owner is all lit up and then I can't concentrate on what I'm watching.

Finally, it's an excuse to be late. If the waiting friend can be contacted, "Just to let you know I'm going to be half an hour late", then somehow being late is therefore OK. No! Just make an effort to arrive on time! Sometimes friends even blame me for sitting alone for twenty minutes when it was they who were late because, they insist, I couldn't be contacted! No, I'm never, ever going to get one!

Reading Comprehension from PRETCO

Task 1

Directions: *After reading the following passage, you will find 5 questions or unfinished statements. For each question or statement there are 4 choices marked A, B, C and D. You should make the correct choice and mark the corresponding letter with a single line through the center. (2006. 06)*

Do you know how to use a mobile phone (手机) without being rude to the people around you?

Talking during a performance irritates (激怒) people. If you are expecting an emergency call, sit near the exit doors and set your phone to vibrate (振动) . When your mobile phone vibrates, you can leave quietly and let the others enjoy the performance.

Think twice before using mobile phones in elevators, museums, churches, or other indoor public places—especially enclosed spaces. Would you want to listen to someone's conversation in these places? Worse yet, how would you feel if a mobile phone rang suddenly during a funeral! It happens more often than you think. Avoid these embarrassing situations by making sure your mobile phone is switched off.

When eating at a restaurant with friends, don't place your mobile phone on the table. This conveys the message that your phone calls are more important than those around you.

Mobile phones have sensitive microphones that allow you to speak at the volume you would on a regular phone. This enables you to speak quietly so that others won't hear the details of your conversation. If you are calling from a noisy area, use your hand to direct your voice into the microphone.

Many people believe that they can't live without their mobile phone. Owning a mobile phone definitely makes life more convenient, but limit your conversations to urgent ones and save the personal calls until you are at home.

1) What should you do when you need to answer a phone call during a performance?
  A. Call back after the performance.
  B. Answer it near the exit door.
  C. Talk outside the exit door.
  D. Speak in a low voice.

2) Putting your mobile phone on a restaurant table may make your friends think _____ .
  A. you prefer to talk to your friends at the table
  B. you value your calls more than your friends
  C. you are enjoying the company of your friends
  D. you are polite and considerate of your friends

3) When you are calling in a noisy area, you are advised to _____.

    A. use a more sensitive microphone

    B. shout loudly into your microphone

    C. go away quietly to continue the phone call

    D. use your hand to help speak into the phone

4) The author implies that the use of mobile phones in such places as museums should be _____.

    A. limited   B. expected   C. discouraged   D. recommended

5) Which of the following is TRUE according to the passage?

    A. You should limit your mobile phone calls to personal affairs.

    B. You should speak quietly into your mobile phone while in a church.

    C. You are supposed to turn off your mobile phone at a funeral.

    D. You are supposed to use your mobile phone as much as possible.

Task 2

Directions: *The following is part of an introduction to a telephone directory. After reading it, you are required to complete the outline below it. You should write your answers briefly (in no more than 3 words) in the blanks correspondingly. (2003. 12)*

A local telephone directory is sometimes called the White Pages. This directory provides an alphabetic listing of names and telephone numbers and other telephone reference information. The front pages usually contain information about area codes; billings; customer service; directory assistance (帮助); local, long-distance, and international calls; time zones; rates; emergency numbers and other items relating to telephone use.

The next section of the telephone directory typically contains the residence listings, or entries of community residents. The third section contains business listings, or entries of local businesses and organizations. In some less populated (人口密集) or rural areas, the residence and business listings may be combined in one section.

Some local directories contain listings of local, state and federal (联邦的) government offices and agencies. These listings might be united into the business listing section, or they may be in a separate section of the phone book. These government listings typically are arranged by the name of the state government and then by departments or agencies.

Local Telephone Directories

Another name: 1) _____

Arrangement of its contents:

Listing of names and telephone numbers: given in an 2) _____ order

Area codes and other useful information: contained in the 3) _____

Residence listings: provided in the 4) _____ section of the directory

Government listings: given either in the business listing section or in a 5) _____

Reading for Fun

The Smart Way to Catch Burglars

It was late and Charlie was about to climb into bed when his wife informed him that there was a light on in their garden shed. Charlie started to go outside to turn off the light but noticed some people in the shed who were busy stealing his things.

He ran back inside right away and called the cops, who asked him "Are there any intruders in your house?" to which Charlie replied "no" and explained his circumstances. The cops told Charlie that all patrol cars were otherwise occupied, and that he should just lock his door and a uniformed cop would be at his house when one was free.

Charlie answered, "Alright," hung up, waited 30 seconds, and then called the cops again. "Hello, I just called a short while ago because there were people stealing things from my shed. I want to let you know that they're not a problem anymore because I've just shot every one of them."

Charlie then hung up the phone. In five short minutes, three patrol cars, a SWAT team, and an ambulance arrived, and of course, the cops caught the burglars in the act. One of the cops snapped at Charlie: "I thought you said that you shot every one of them!" "I thought you said there were no patrol cars free!" Charlie answered.

Unit 6
Renewing Educational Concept

Passage A   Nature School

Nature is the greatest teacher in nursery schools of Scandinavia. All across Scandinavia small children are running wild! From Lapland to Jutland, you will see flocks of youngsters chasing through meadows and woodland, with mud-spattered faces and small rucksacks on their backs. You will find them splashing in streams, crawling through the undergrowth, clambering up trees or sitting quietly on a log eating a sandwich. These are children from one of the many "naturbornehaver" (nature kindergartens) that are currently mushrooming up all over Norway, Denmark, Sweden and Finland.

Yes, this is the pedagogical hit of our time—the startlingly simple concept of taking children out in nature as often as possible, for as long as possible, in all weathers and in all seasons. And research shows that these "nature" children gain far more than rosy cheeks and bright eyes; for it is now evident that nature nursery school children are socially, physically and intellectually at an advantage over their contemporaries in conventional nursery schools. No wonder then, that the rate of growth in this area of childcare is phenomenal. In Denmark, nearly all county councils now have one or two such schools.

Although there are many variations on the theme, nature nursery schools are most often based in a forest. A forest gives the perfect frame for a child's natural physical development. When a child experiences the freedom and stimulation offered by the forest, the result is a more balanced and peaceful child who is able to deal with social and intellectual challenges far more effectively.

The forest offers a multitude of learning opportunities. Children can run around as much as they want; noise is absorbed by the immensity of the sky. Children can use their bodies to the full; climbing, swinging, crawling, carrying, leaping. What's more, the forest is filled with an abundance of playthings: a stick transforms into a horse or into a baton to conduct a brass band. Imagination can literally run wild through the trees.

For these children, the world is teeming with life: slugs and beetles, wild raspberries and hazelnuts, woodpeckers and jays. What better way could there be to learn about animals, plants and the changing of the seasons? What more effective way to teach children about basic ecological concerns, when they arise so spontaneously and in such a genuine context?

Most often, such nursery schools are "green". They buy organic and environmentally-friendly products, and work with the concept of environmental sustainability, e.g. composting and energy-saving. In giving children a chance to establish a meaningful, intimate and responsible relationship with the natural world, it must be a regular daily practice for them to touch the earth, to hear birdsong, to collect berries and mushrooms and to get to know animals and plants. In wind, rain, snow and shine, let the children run wild!

Ⓝew Words

1. abundance	n.	大量，丰盛
2. band	n.	乐队
3. baton	n.	（乐队）指挥棒
4. brass	n.	铜管乐器
5. challenge	n.	挑战
6. chase	v.	追赶，追逐
7. clamber	v.	攀爬，攀登
8. compost	v.	把（植物、树叶等）制成堆肥
9. contemporary	n.	同一时代或同一年龄的人
10. conventional	a.	传统的
11. council	n.	议会，政务会
12. ecological	a.	生态的
13. effectively	ad.	有效地
14. evident	a.	明显的，显然的
15. flock	n.	一大群人
16. immensity	n.	巨大，广大
17. intellectually	ad.	需要或使用智力（地）
18. intimate	a.	亲近的，亲密的
19. literally	ad.	真正地，确实地
20. log	n.	圆木
21. multitude	n.	众多，大量
22. phenomenal	a.	了不起的，非凡的
23. splash	v.	溅水，泼湿
24. sustainability	n.	可持续
25. teem	v.	充满

Notes

1. Scandinavia: 斯堪的纳维亚，北欧一地区，包括挪威、丹麦和瑞典，有时还包括冰岛、芬兰和法罗群岛。

   Lapland: 拉普兰，北欧一地区，指拉普人居住的地方，包括挪威、瑞典、芬兰等国的北部和俄罗斯的科拉半岛。

   Jutland: 日德兰半岛，位于北海和波罗的海之间。

2. Yes, this is the pedagogical hit of our time—the startlingly simple concept of taking children out in nature as often as possible, for as long as possible, in all weathers and in all seasons.

   是的，这是风靡我们这个时代的教学方法———一种极其朴素的观念，即带孩子们到大自然中去，不管什么天气，无论什么季节，越经常越好，时间越久越好。

   pedagogical hit: 流行的教学法，hit在这里意为"风行，流行的事物"，例如，Her new film is quite a hit.

   startlingly: 惊人地，令人震惊地，例如，She is startlingly beautiful.

3. For these children, the world is teeming with life: slugs and beetles, wild raspberries and hazelnuts, woodpeckers and jays.

   对这些孩子来说，世界充满着生机：蛞蝓、甲虫、覆盆子、榛子、啄木鸟和松鸦。

   teem with sth.: 充满（人或动物等），例如，Times Square was teeming with theater-goers.

4. What more effective way to teach children about basic ecological concerns, when they arise so spontaneously and in such a genuine context?

   在真实的大自然环境中，基本生态意识自然而然地浮现在孩子们心中，还有比这更有效的教学方法吗？

   spontaneously: 自然地，自发地，它的形容词形式是spontaneous，例如，spontaneous applause/cheers, 自发的鼓掌/欢呼

   genuine context: 真实情景，真实背景

5. Most often, such nursery schools are "green". They buy organic and environmentally-friendly products, and work with the concept of environmental sustainability, e.g. composting and energy-saving.

   这些幼儿园一般都是"绿色环保"的。它们购买有机和环保产品，按照可持续发展的理念来运作，比如制作堆肥和节约能源等。

Exercises

1. Choose the best answer.

1) Why are there so many nature nursery schools in Scandinavia?

   A. Because in these schools, children can chase, splash, crawl or clamber.

   B. Because teachers in these schools allow children to run wild.

   C. Because nature is regarded as the greatest teacher to small children.

D. Because a lot of nature nursery schools are appearing more rapidly than expected.

2) What is the main advantage of nature nursery schools according to the reading text?

A. Children in nature nursery schools become much wiser than their contemporaries.

B. Children in nature nursery schools gain rosy cheeks and bright eyes.

C. The growth rate of nature nursery schools is very phenomenal.

D. Children in nature nursery schools are more competent socially, physically and intellectually.

3) What is the basic element of a nature nursery school?

A. Teachers.

B. A forest.

C. Variations on the theme.

D. A nature kindergarten.

4) In the author's opinion, the children's ability to effectively handle social and intellectual challenges _____.

A. grows out of their experience of freedom and stimulation offered by the forest

B. is the result of a more balanced and peaceful environment

C. develops with an abundance of playthings in the forest

D. helps them to get a multitude of learning opportunities and use their bodies to the full

5) The best way to teach children basic ecological concerns is to _____.

A. take them out in nature as often as possible

B. send them to nature nursery schools

C. let them have a regular daily practice, such as touching the earth, hearing birdsong, so on and so forth

D. put them in wind, rain, snow and shine and let them run wild

2. Complete the statements that follow the questions.

1) Why are nature nursery schools mushrooming up in Scandinavia?

Because children in nature nursery schools are _____ superior to their contemporaries in conventional nursery schools.

2) Why does the author say that forest is often the basis of a nature nursery school?

Because it offers _____ for a child's natural physical development.

3) Why do we say nature nursery schools are "green"?

Because these schools buy _____ and work with the concept of environmental sustainability.

4) How can we help children to establish a meaningful, intimate and responsible relationship with nature?

We should allow children _____ in the natural world.

5) What's the main idea of the reading text?

Nature _____ to children.

3. Match the following words with the definitions below and then fill in the blanks with their proper forms.

concept	evident	chase	stimulation	council
flock	context	theme	variation	contemporary
abundance	balance	swing	absorb	intellectual

1) (*verb*) to quickly follow sb. or sth. in order to catch them

The local police have been _____ the murderer for half a month.

2) (*noun*) a large group of the same kind of people

Visitors came in _____ to the museum which was open to the public for free.

3) (*adjective*) clear to the eyes or mind

It is _____ that the 2008 Beijing Olympic Games and Paralympic Games have both been a great success.

4) (*adjective*) relating to the ability to think in an intelligent way

Playing chess is usually considered as a(n) _____ game.

5) (*noun*) a group of people that are chosen to make rules, laws or decisions, or to give advice

A _____ of elders governs the tribe.

6) (*noun*) a very large quantity of sth.

Fruits and vegetables grew in _____ on the island.

7) (*noun*) the situation, events, or information that are related to sth., and that help you to understand it better

These changes must be seen in their historical and social _____.

8) (*noun*) general idea or notion

It is relatively difficult for some old people to get rid of the old _____ of living.

9) (*noun*) anything that encourages sth. to happen, develop, or improve

The successful accomplishment of *Shenzhou* VI space flight is a great _____ to *Shenzhou* VII mission.

10) (*verb*) to keep or put one in a state of balance

Mr. Smith keeps healthy by sticking to physical exercise and well _____ his diet.

11) (*verb*) to take in or suck in

Dry sand _____ water quickly.

12) (*noun*) someone who lives or lived at the same time as another

Shelley and Keats were _____.

13) (*verb*) to move forwards and backwards or in a curve

The wind pushed the door open, then caused it to _____ shut.

14) (*noun*) the main subject of sth. such as a book, speech, exhibition or discussion

Love and honor are the main _____ of the book.

15) (*noun*) a difference or change from the usual form of sth.

There are wide regional _____ in house prices.

Reading Skills

⑨ast Reading

快速阅读

　　快速阅读是英语阅读中的一个重要技巧，要求读者在规定的时间内，快速、准确地找到有关信息，完成相应的答题任务。快速阅读的测试时间一般较短。大学英语四级考试中的快速阅读测试，要求考生在15分钟内阅读一篇1000-1200词左右的文章，并解答文章后相应的测试题。在高职高专学生参加的英语应用能力考试（PRETCO）中，虽然阅读理解部分没有明显标注"快速阅读"字样，但如果具备高效、快速的文章阅读能力，同样对解题大有裨益。

　　快速阅读可以是多种阅读技巧的综合运用。本书前面各单元中所介绍过的各种阅读技巧，如篇章预览、从上、下文猜测词义、寻找主题句、略读、查读等等，都能应用于快速阅读之中。为了有效完成快速阅读，一般要注意以下几点：

　　1. 集中精力阅读。切忌一心二用，一边阅读，一边分神想其他事情，以致影响阅读的速度和准确性。

2. 快速阅读时，努力做到以句子为单位，按照较长的意群来进行阅读。句子与句子之间，段落与段落之间的停顿间隙尽可能缩短。虽然不能做到一目十行，一眼看过去的词汇也要尽量多些，以加快阅读的速度。

3. 快速阅读时，手指不要指着文章逐字逐句读，也不要出声读或在脑子里默读，更不要返回到刚刚读过的内容，把它再读一遍。因为，这些不良的阅读习惯会极大地影响阅读的速度。

4. 快速阅读要求较高，阅读者必须具备一定的背景知识、词汇量、语言基础和一定的阅读技能。只有这样，快速阅读才有可能比较顺利地进行。所以，我们在平时的学习中，要注重积累，注意实践，把所学的知识运用到实际阅读中去。

[例]

To: All Employees

From: Berry E. Silver, President

Date: Oct. 22, 2004

Subject: Our goals for the next year

Marketing and Sales

Our present sales program has helped us to improve our sales by slightly over 15%, but I am setting a goal of a 25% increase in sales for the next year. To help make this goal possible, I am announcing today the expansion (扩大) of our Marketing Department.

Research and Development (R&D)

Any company in our business must make great efforts to develop new and better products. Our R&D will certainly make us more competitive. But creative ideas do not come from only R&D departments; they also come from the creative thinking and participation of all employees. One way we have begun to collect the suggestions of our employees is through our new computerized network.

Human Resources

Our company's most valuable resources are its employees. In the years ahead I would like to see our efforts doubled in on-the-job training. To achieve this goal I have asked Barbara Johnson to head a new department, Human Resources and Employee Development, which will coordinate (协调) a company-wide effort.

Memo

Subject: Goals for the next year

Marketing and Sales:

- Goal set: to reach a 1) _____ in sales;

- Measure to be taken: to expand the 2) _____;

Research and Development (R&D):

- Goal set: to encourage the employees' participation;

- Channel to collect suggestions: the new 3) _____ ;

Human Resources:

- Requirement set: to double the efforts in 4) _____ ;

- Measure to be taken: to appoint Barbara Johnson to head 5) _____ .

这是一份备忘录。题目的设置形式虽然不是快速阅读中常见的正、误判断题，而是填空题，但也可以用快速阅读的方法来做。填空题的题干往往都是原文语句的同义解释，所以，只要抓住关键词语和信息，结合略读、查读等技巧进行快速阅读，很快就能完成这些填空题。下文斜体部分为本题答案。

1) Goal set: 文章第1段清楚地写明了来年的增长目标，*25% increase* in sales for the next year.

2) Measure to be taken: 文章第1段同样阐述了实现目标的途径，the expansion of our *Marketing Department*.

3) Channel to collect suggestions: 抓住关键词to collect suggestions快速浏览文章，即可在第2段的最后一句话中找到答案，即through our new *computerized network*.

4) Requirement set: 抓住关键词to double the efforts，就可以在第3段开头的第2句话中找到这一题的答案，即to see our efforts doubled in *on-the-job training*.

5) Measure to be taken: 在原文的最后一句话中，to achieve this goal提示我们答案就是I have asked Barbara Johnson to head *a new department*.

Exercises

Read fast the following application letter and complete the outline below it briefly (in no more than 3 words for each blank).

Dear Mr. Williams,

Your advertisement in this morning's paper for manager of public relations appeals to me. I found the wording of your advertisement quite attractive with emphasis on leadership, initiative, and flexibility. And my experience and qualifications indicate that I am the person you are seeking.

The enclosed resume indicates my experience in the area of public relations and management communications. I am quite familiar with the kinds of issues and problems that you have to deal with.

I'd like to draw your attention to Page 2 of my resume, on which I describe my concept of public relations. And I am most eager to put this concept into practice to prove it to you.

Although I have been very happy with my present employer and colleagues, I am more willing to join your company where I can assume even broader responsibility.

I am free to travel and open to relocation. I would welcome the opportunity to meet you and to further discuss how I may benefit your organization. Please call me at 0411-89726374 to arrange an interview at your earliest convenience.

Sincerely yours,

Stephen Smith

An Application Letter

Applicant: 1) _____

Position applied for: the manager of 2) _____

Requirements emphasized in the ad: • leadership

• initiative

• 3) _____

Expectation of the applicant: to assume 4) _____

Contact telephone number: 0411-89726374

Purpose of the letter: asking for 5) _____

Passage B   The School of Rock

Read the passage and judge whether the following statements are true (T) or false (F).

1) Dewey is keen on rock and roll and has his own band organized with his friends.

2) As a substitute, Dewey goes to a primary school, which is called The School of Rock.

3) When Dewey puts forward his suggestion that "his band" need a field trip, the principal doesn't agree at first, but later she is tricked into giving her allowance.

4) The song the band decides to play on the concert is written by Dewey himself.

5) Dewey has to perform with his students in the parents' meeting before he goes to the concert, otherwise he will have no field trip.

6) Ned gets pay from Horace Green School, which makes him puzzled.

7) Ned tells his girlfriend that Dewey is a impostor. Thus, Dewey's secret is let out.

8) Dewey's band members forgive Dewey without hesitation and decide to finish the "project" of rock show.

9) The performance by Dewey's band is a great success and ranks first in the Battle of the Bands.

10) At last, Dewey is lucky enough to be invited to run the band in Horace Green School.

Dewey is a crazy rock'n'roll guitar player in a band. He decides to have his own band but it is all to no avail (没有效果) in spite of his efforts. However, things begin to look up (好转) one day when Horace Green School, an elementary school's principal Rosalie Mullins calls in asking Ned, his only friend, to substitute (代替) a teacher who suddenly falls ill.

Pretending to be Ned, Dewey comes to the school driving his van loaded with the band instruments. Assigning roles and positions to every boy and girl, Dewey gets his own rock band organized. The

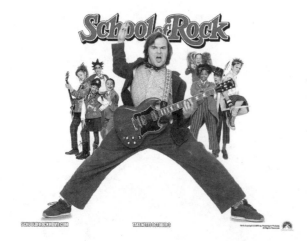

kids name the band the School of Rock. Dewey suggests that his class need a field trip (校外考察旅行), but the principal Rosalie rejects the proposal because Dewey is a substitute.

To get to the audition (试演) for the famous Battle of the Bands, the class have to sneak out. Dewey tries to persuade the contest manager to put them on the list.

From the colleagues Dewey learns that Rosalie is not always rigid. She got drunk at the alumni party (校友聚会). So, after work, Dewey invites Rosalie to a bar. He orders two big glasses of beer. When Rosalie is a little drunk, Dewey chooses her favorite song from the jukebox (投币式点唱机) and Rosalie gets greatly excited. When they sing the song together, Dewey tells her that the concert he's going to take the class to will be very educational. And in drunkenness, Rosalie agrees to the field trip proposal.

In the next class, Dewey encourages Zack, the talented guitarist of the band, to develop a rock song. The whole class love it and they decide to play it in the Battle of the Bands. When Dewey mentions the field trip again, the now sober Rosalie is reluctant. After Dewey's hard persuasion, she finally agrees but under the condition that he has to attend the parents' meeting and give them a presentation. Back in the apartment, Ned tells Dewey that strangely he has received a check of $12,000 from Horace Green School. Dewey has to tell Ned the truth before he hurries back to school for the parents' night. When Patty, Ned's girlfriend, finds out what Dewey did, she calls the police.

As Dewey is explaining about his teaching to the parents, the police take Patty and Ned to the class and disclose him on the spot. The parents get angry and blame Rosalie for employing an impostor (冒牌货). The kids, however, after a little discussion, decide to forgive Dewey and finish the "project" of rock show. Ned, out of his own passion for rock, also decides to go to the show despite Patty's objection. The result is that they both rush to the "concert".

Zack's song turns out to be a huge success and wins long-lasting applauses. Even the parents are thrilled to see the wonderful performance. Though the top award is given to another band, the audience think the School of Rock is the best. Upon the audience's request, the band gives an encore (加演)—a song written by Dewey.

Everyone has learned something from the incident. Passion and interest are more important than rigid methods and dull knowledge. One should learn or teach according to their own aptitude. Dewey gets officially employed as a teacher at Horace Green School for "after school program".

Reading Comprehension from PRETCO

Task 1

Directions: *After reading the following passage, you will find 5 questions or unfinished statements. For each question or statement there are 4 choices marked A, B, C and D. You should make the correct choice and mark the corresponding letter with a single line through the center. (2002. 06)*

In many countries, such as France, Greece and Japan, it is often more difficult for students to pass the college entrance exams than to do the course work when they are actually in college, and students who don't have much money are at a disadvantage. Students prepare for these tests for years in advance. Often, students attend a private school at night to get ready for them. These private schools are usually expensive. If their families don't have much money, students can't attend, and they might not pass the entrance exams without this extra preparation.

In contrast, students can easily get into an American or Canadian college at least more easily than in other countries. American students take an entrance exam called the SAT (the Scholastic Aptitude Test). However, colleges do not consider only SAT scores. They also consider a student's grades and activities throughout high school. A student who has done well in high school will probably get into college.

What happens when a student finally enters a college or university? Students in China, South Korea, or Japan might find their college studies easier than high school work. On the other hand, when American or Canadian students begin college, many of them discover that they need to work very hard and study seriously for the first time in their lives especially if they plan to go to graduate school.

1) In France and Greece, students find that _____.
   A. they have to do extra preparation to pass the college entrance exams
   B. private schools are inexpensive
   C. course work in college is more difficult than college entrance exams
   D. college entrance exams are more difficult than course work in college

2) From the first paragraph we can see that before entering college, students must _____.
   A. pass the entrance exams
   B. study in private schools
   C. earn enough money
   D. do some course work

3) In America, colleges usually take in new students according to _____.
   A. students' grades and activities in high school only
   B. students' SAT scores only
   C. both students' SAT scores and records in high school
   D. students' objectives of academic study

4) In North America, college students _____.
   A. study harder than they did in high school
   B. study as hard as they did in high school
   C. find college studies easier than high school work
   D. find it easier to go to graduate school

5) This passage is mainly about _____.
   A. advantages of college study in North America
   B. differences in college education in different countries
   C. American higher education
   D. higher education in general

Task 2

Directions: *After reading the following introduction to the course on First Certificate in English, you are required to complete the outline below it. You should write your answers briefly (in no more than 3 words) in the blanks correspondingly. (2003. 06)*

English for Cambridge Examination

This course prepares non-native speakers for the internationally recognized First Certificate in English.

Syllabus (课程大纲)

Speaking skills are taught as part of an integrated approach. Special emphasis is placed on the ability to communicate successfully at all levels. Listening skills are also taught as part of an integrated approach. Extensive use is made of our modern language laboratory and video self-access center.

Grammar practice is an essential part of the preparation for the examination. Students are introduced to word processing on computers.

Integrated into our basic syllabus for speaking, listening and reading are regular classes on British life and institutions including the legal system, politics and the press. Literary (文学) texts form a part of all courses.

Careers and future study

The FCE is an intermediate qualification internationally recognized in commerce, industry and higher education.

Admission

Application—refer direct to the Language Center, University Brighton, Falmer, Brighton BN1 9PH for details and application forms.

Contact

Course leader: Martin Wilson 211-0934398

Training Course for FCE

Intended for: 1) _____ of English to obtain the internationally recognized

First Certificate in English

Skills to be trained: speaking, 2) _____ and reading

Teaching aids available: modern 3) _____ and 4) _____ self-access center

Contact person: 5) _____

Reading for Fun

A Dead Rabbit

This guy comes home from work one day to find his dog with the neighbor's pet rabbit in his mouth. The rabbit is very dead and the guy panics. He thinks the neighbors are going to hate him forever, so he takes the dirty, chewed-up rabbit into the house, gives it a bath, blow-dries its fur, and puts the rabbit back into the cage at the neighbor's house, hoping that they will think it died of natural causes.

A few days later, the neighbor is outside and asks the guy, "Did you hear that Fluffy died?" The guy stumbles around and says, "Um…no…um…what happened?" The neighbor replies, "We just found him dead in his cage one day, but the weird thing is that the day after we buried him we went outside and someone dug him up, gave him a bath and put him back into the cage. There must be some real sick people out there!"

Unit 7
Exploring Outer Space

Passage A *Shenzhou* VII **Ready for Historic Task**

The team that developed *Shenzhou* VII, China's third manned spacecraft, will begin the final test at Jiuquan Satellite Launch Center in a few days. The research and development team of China Aerospace Science and Technology Corporation will set out for Jiuquan early this month.

Shenzhou VII's functions and performance fulfill the comprehensive requirements of the space program. *Shenzhou* VII manned spacecraft is expected to be ready for launch in October. It will be carried by the *Long March*-IIF carrier rocket, which is set to complete its third manned space mission this year and its seventh mission overall.

The mission of *Shenzhou* VII is aimed at mastering two key technologies necessary for setting up a space laboratory or station, where spacecraft can dock and perform extra-vehicular activities.

Shenzhou VII will be launched with a crew of three astronauts. Shortly before the spacewalk, two of the astronauts will enter the orbital module at the front of the spacecraft. The hatch linking the orbital module to the descent module, containing the third astronaut, will be sealed soon after the crew splits in two.

The orbital module will house the extra-vehicular activity suits during the flight, and the two astronauts will spend a considerable amount of time checking the suits before they don them. Next, there will be more checks once the astronauts are inside their suits.

The air pressure inside the orbital module will be gradually reduced to vacuum, and the large circular outer hatch on the side of the orbital module will then be swung inwards. One astronaut will then carefully step outside the module, clutching handrails on the outside of the spacecraft, to become China's first spacewalker.

There are two kinds of spacewalk. One is when the astronaut is tied to the spaceship and the other is a free walk, where they are unattached. During the *Shenzhou* VII mission, a spacewalker will conduct a

free walk. The early spacewalks conducted by Russia and the United States were not free walks. To ensure that the mission is a success, experts have prepared plans to deal with more than 30 emergency situations to guarantee the astronauts' safety.

The mission differs from previous ones in three ways. First, it will carry out extra-vehicular activities, which will put the homemade airlock module and space suits to strict tests in space for the first time. Secondly, the three astronauts will stay in *Shenzhou* VII for up to five days, testing its rated capacity. Thirdly, experiments will be conducted with new satellite communication technology.

China has initiated a step-by-step approach for its astronauts. This began with the single-person *Shenzhou* V flight in 2003 of 14 orbits, followed by the two-person voyage of *Shenzhou* VI in 2005 lasting 5 days, and now the coming mission. The exact day that the three-person crew will take off in October is yet to be announced, but there has been talk about broadcasting the spacewalk live on television when it happens.

Yuanwang VI, an ocean-going tracking ship, has been delivered for service from Shanghai to participate in the *Shenzhou* VII flight and to assist in the spacewalk. It joins its sister ship, *Yuanwang* V, to take part in maritime space surveying and mission control operations.

An academician of the Chinese Academy of Engineering and researcher of the China Spaceflight Technology Research Institute—credited as chief designer of China's first five *Shenzhou* spaceships and chief consultant for *Shenzhou* VI and *Shenzhou* VII—has been quoted as saying that plans are already underway for *Shenzhou* VIII and *Shenzhou* IX and that the intervals between each launch will become shorter.

New Words

1. academician	*n.*	院士
2. capacity	*n.*	容积，容量，容纳力
3. clutch	*v.*	抓紧，紧握
4. comprehensive	*a.*	综合的，全面的
5. considerable	*a.*	大量的
6. consultant	*n.*	顾问
7. corporation	*n.*	公司
8. crew	*n.*	全体机组人员
9. descent	*n.*	下降，降落
10. dock	*v.*	宇宙飞船在太空对接
11. don	*v.*	穿（衣）
12. emergency	*n.*	紧急情况
13. fulfill	*v.*	符合（要求，条件）
14. guarantee	*v.*	保证，保障

15. handrail	*n.*	手把，扶手
16. hatch	*n.*	舱口
17. initiate	*v.*	开始，发动
18. maritime	*a.*	海上的，海事的
19. mission	*n.*	任务，特殊使命
20. module	*n.*	（太空船）舱
21. orbital	*a.*	轨道的
22. seal	*v.*	密封
23. split	*v.*	分开，使分开（成为几个部分）
24. swing	*v.*	（使）旋转，转动
25. unattached	*a.*	不连接的

Notes

1. Jiuquan Satellite Launch Center: 酒泉卫星发射中心，又称东风航天城，地处戈壁，是中国科学卫星，技术试验卫星和运载火箭的发射试验基地之一。

2. the *Long March*-IIF carrier rocket: "长征" 二号F型运载火箭，用于发射 "神舟" 七号载人飞船。火箭全长58.3米，起飞重量479.8吨，由四个液体火箭助推器和芯一级、二级、整流罩、逃逸塔组成，包括控制系统、故障检测系统、遥测系统、外测安全系统、推进剂利用系统、附加系统和地面设备等10个分系统。可靠性指标从原来的0.97提升到0.98，航天员安全性指标达到0.997。乘坐的舒适性也得到了进一步改善。

3. *Yuanwang* VI, an ocean-going tracking ship, has been delivered for service from Shanghai to participate in the *Shenzhou* VII flight and to assist in the spacewalk.
   远洋测量船 "远望" 六号，已从上海出发参与和帮助 "神七" 飞行和太空行走的任务。
   Yuanwang VI: "远望" 六号测量船，属于中国卫星海上测控部。2008年9月19日，和其他四艘测量船——"远望" 一号、二号、三号、五号一起，顺利到达太平洋、大西洋预定海域，执行 "神舟" 七号载人飞船海上测控任务。

Exercises

1. Choose the best answer.

1) What is the aim of the *Shenzhou* VII mission?

   A. To send three astronauts up into outer space.

   B. To fulfill the comprehensive requirements of the space program.

   C. To grasp two vitally important technologies needed for establishing a space laboratory or station.

   D. To test the *Long March*-IIF carrier rocket and the rated capacity of the spacecraft.

2) What does the phrase "extra-vehicular activities" (Line 2, Para. 3) mean?

A. Additional activities for the three astronauts.

B. Activities done outside the spacecraft.

C. Activities that must be performed according to the plan.

D. Everyday activities the three astronauts should complete.

3) Where will the spacewalker stay before he makes the spacewalk?

A. The orbital module.

B. The descent module.

C. The hatch linking the orbital module to the descent module.

D. At the front of the spacecraft.

4) In which ways does the *Shenzhou* VII mission differ from previous ones?

A. It will carry out extra-vehicular activities.

B. It will conduct experiments using new satellite communication technology.

C. Three astronauts will stay in *Shenzhou* VII for up to five days.

D. All of the above.

5) Which of the following is the best to express the significance of the *Shenzhou* VII mission?

A. It is one small step for the astronaut, but a huge achievement for China's aerospace industry.

B. It is one small step for the astronaut, but an important progress for human civilization.

C. It is one small step for a man, but a big step for the world's aerospace industry.

D. It is one small step for a man, but a significant advance for world peace.

2. Complete the statements that follow the questions.

1) How will the astronaut step outside the module?

He will step out of the module carefully _____ handrails on the outside of the spacecraft.

2) When will the astronauts check their extra-vehicular suits?

They will check their suits _____.

3) How many kinds of spacewalk are mentioned in the text and what are they?

There are _____ kinds of spacewalk; they are _____.

4) What measures have been prepared to guarantee the astronauts' safety?

Experts have worked out plans to _____ more than 30 emergency situations.

5) What is the role of *Yuanwang* VI, the ocean-going tracking ship, according to the text?

To _____ the *Shenzhou* VII mission.

3. Match the following words with the definitions below and then fill in the blanks with their proper forms.

crew   approach   descent   guarantee   split

vehicular   mission   seal   voyage   consultant

considerable   capacity   initiate   emergency   interval

1) (*verb*) to promise that sth. will certainly happen or be done

If you purchase our products, our company will _____ satisfactory after-sale services.

2) (*noun*) an important job that someone has been given to do especially when they are sent to another place

It is the first time he is sent to that country on a diplomatic _____, and he feels a little worried.

3) (*adjective*) related to vehicles

The notice says the bridge will be under repair next week, so it is closed to _____ traffic from today.

4) (*noun*) all the persons working on a ship, aircraft, train, etc.

This early morning came the sad news that an air crash happened last night and all the passengers and _____ were killed.

5) (*noun*) the process of going down

The climber had great difficulty in making his _____ from the snowy mountain.

6) (*verb*) to fasten or close sth. tightly

The fruit jars must be well _____ to prevent air from going in so as to keep the fruit fresh.

7) (*verb*) to break into two or more parts

For the purpose of the survey, we've _____ the town into four areas.

8) (*adjective*) great in amount or size

The house was bought at _____ expense.

9) (*noun*) time between two events or two parts of an action

No. 5 bus used to come every ten minutes. Now the _____ has been shortened to every two minutes.

10) (*noun*) ability to contain things

The National Stadium, which has a seating _____ of about 90 thousand, along with the Water cube are two architectural wonders of our country.

11) (*noun*) serious happening or situation which needs quick action to deal with

This medical device is designed for patients to use in an _____.

12) (*verb*) to arrange for sth. important to start, such as an official process or a new plan

The committee held the conference in order to _____ the plan of reducing environmental pollution.

13) (*noun*) movement towards or near to sth.

Usually the _____ of the terminal examinations gives students worry and sleeplessness.

14) (*noun*) a long journey in a ship

The Titanic hit the iceberg and sank on its maiden _____ .

15) (*noun*) someone who has a lot of experience and whose job is to give advice

After his retirement, Mr. Beamer was invited to be a _____ of the company.

Reading Skills

Sequencing
顺序阅读

　　每件事情的发生都不是孤立、偶然的。一件事可能发生在另一件事之前或之后或同时发生。二者之间的关联或顺序可能是按时间先后、逻辑关系，或是因果关系等进行排列。一篇条理清晰，结构严密，说服力强的文章必然要遵循一定的关联或顺序。阅读时，如何按照文章顺序进行理解呢？一般的文章通常有以下几种行文方式：

　　1. 按时间的先后顺序进行描写，如历史事件，名人轶事等。

　　2. 按空间顺序进行描写，如名胜古迹，场景介绍等。

　　3. 按从一般到个别或从个别到一般的顺序进行描写。前者的顺序，作者通常把具有概括意义的主题句放在段落开头，然后提供材料进行论证；后者的顺序与前者相反，作者先列出材料，然后逐步分析引出结论，把具有概括意义的主题句放在段末。在议论文中常可见这两种写作手法。

4. 按重要性递减或递增的顺序进行描写。前者把重要的内容放在文章前面，把次要的内容放在文章后面。后者的描写顺序则相反，目的在于逐步引起读者的兴趣，最后达到引人入胜的高潮。一些表达时间和序列概念的介词、连词、副词及一些短语往往能够帮助我们判定文中事情发生的顺序，如first, then, afterward, so far等。

[例] In the middle of the rectangular-shaped courtyard, stood three magnolia trees, all in full bloom. A little girl was hopping among them, now gazing at a bud, now collecting fallen petals. Under one of the trees stood her parents, who, while keeping one eye on her, were examining the milk-white blossoms with great interest and admiration. In front of another tree a young couple, fresh and bright as the flowers, were posing for a picture. At one end of the courtyard, a group of youngsters had gathered behind an artist painting a flourishing limb. At the opposite end, a few elderly men and women stood admiring the leafless flowering trees.

此文描述了一个长方形庭院，观察点是树。作者从院子中的树开始描写，以树为中心，描述树上树下树前树后的情景，把树的静态和人的动态（小女孩在树间跳来跳去，年轻夫妇准备拍照等）相结合，然后再描述庭院的两端。所有这一切使人感到院内呈现一派生气盎然的景象。显然，这是有关空间顺序的描写。

空间位置型段落的特点是描述，是以语言的形式再现客观世界或表现想象中的世界。要描述，就离不开具体的细节。只有细节才能表现出人、物或景的平面或立体联系。阅读时，注意把握人、物、景的不同细节在空间中所占据的位置及其相互间的平面联系和立体关系，就能在脑海中迅速勾勒出一幅清晰的画面，从而加深对文章的理解。

[例] English language is full of words that have gradually changed their meanings. One example is the word graft. The verb graft first meant merely "to work". English people once used the word in such expressions as "Where are you grafting?" meaning "Where are you working?" From this perfectly respectable meaning, the word has gradually changed. Today graft refers to illegal gains won by dishonest politicians; while in medicine it refers to a portion of living tissue surgically transplanted from one part of an individual to another or from one individual to another with a view to its adhesion and growth.

此文采用的是从一般到具体的写作手法。作者先提出一个普遍现象，然后举例进行论证。首句"English is full of words that have gradually changed their meanings."陈述这样一个事实：英语中有许多词，其意义逐渐发生了变化。example是语言信号词，提示我们作者要以graft为例具体说明这种变化。所以，从一般到具体的例证型段落都具有说明性的、说服人的性质，段落往往带语言信号词。例证型段落的首句通常是概括句，提出命题，而后用实例说明这个命题。

Exercises

1. Rearrange the following sentences into a coherent paragraph.

a. There are differences because there are ants of very many kinds—more than 15,000 kinds in fact.

b. But in general each kind has ants of three main types: queens, males, workers.

c. Human beings are extremely interested in the study of ants.

d. Our dictionary tells us that the ant is a social insect.

e. The societies are not all exactly the same.

f. That means that ants live in societies in which they depend on one another.

g. The more we study them, the more they seem to be like ourselves.

( )→( )→( )→( )→( )→( )→( )

2. Read the following paragraph and choose the best answer.

People do not analyze every problem they meet. Sometimes they try to remember solution from the last time they had a similar problem.

They often accept the opinions or ideas of other people. Other times they begin to act without thinking; they try to find a solution by trial and error. However, when all these methods fail, the person with a problem has to start analyzing. There are six stages in analyzing a problem.

First the person must recognize that there is a problem. For example, Sam's bicycle is broken and he cannot ride it to class as he usually does. Sam must see that there is a problem with his bicycle.

Next the thinker must define the problem. Before Sam can repair his bicycle, he must find the reason why it does not work. For instance, he must determine if the problem is with the gears, the brakes or the frame. He must make his problem more specific.

Now the person must look for the information that will make the problem clearer and lead to possible solutions. For instance, suppose Sam decides that his bike does not work because there is something wrong with the gear wheels. At this time, he can look up in his bicycle repair book and read about gears. He can talk to his friends at the bike shop. He can look at his gear carefully.

After studying the problem, the person should have several suggestions for a possible solution. Take Sam as an illustration again. His suggestion might be: put oil on the gear wheels; buy new gear wheels and replace the old ones; tighten or loosen the gear wheels.

Eventually one suggestion seems to be the solution to the problem. Sometimes the final idea comes very suddenly because the thinker suddenly sees something new or sees something in a new way. Sam, for example, suddenly sees that there is a piece of chewing gum (口香糖) between the gear wheels. He immediately realizes the solution to his problem: he must clean the gear wheels.

Finally the solution is tested. Sam cleans the gear wheels and finds that afterwards his bicycle works perfectly. In short, he has solved the problem.

1) Which of the following would best summarize the main idea of the passage?
   A. Suggestions for repairing Sam's bicycle.
   B. Sam's problem with his bicycle.
   C. Possible ways to solve a problem.
   D. Necessity of analysis for solving problems.

2) In analyzing a problem people must follow all the following steps except _____.
   A. trying to solve it regardless of the result
   B. recognizing and defining the problem
   C. getting information to make the problem clearer
   D. having suggestions for a possible solution

3) The author's purpose of citing Sam's broken bicycle as an example is to _____.
   A. suggest the possible problems of his bicycle
   B. tell us how to analyze a problem
   C. illustrate the ways of repairing a bicycle
   D. show us how to solve a problem

4) Sam gets his broken bicycle work perfectly by _____.
   A. analyzing the problem
   B. asking his friends for help
   C. reading a bicycle repair book
   D. cleaning the dirty wheel

5) Which of the following statements is NOT TRUE?
   A. People often accept other people's opinions.
   B. People sometimes learn from their past experience.
   C. People don't have to analyze the problems they meet.
   D. People may fail to solve some problems they meet.

Passage B *Shenzhou* VII Mission Marks the Maiden Spacewalk by Chinese Astronauts

Read the passage and judge whether the following statements are true (T) or false (F).

1) The mission of *Shenzhou* VII has drawn the world's special attention because it is the first time for China to conduct a spacewalk.

2) Shortly before the spacewalk, two astronauts remained in the capsule while the third entered the orbital module to conduct EVA.

3) The three astronauts flew in space for about 3 days and nights before they returned to the earth.

4) China is the third country capable of sending astronauts into space. The other two are the United States and the United Kingdom.

5) Up untill now, China has sent six astronauts into outer space.

6) The spacesuits are one of the most important things for astronauts in their space flight.

7) The astronaut who stayed in the capsule wore the spacesuit which was made in Russia.

8) The training program the astronauts received is tough and unbearable to ordinary people.

9) China now has 14 would-be astronauts for the future space programs.

10) The success of *Shenzhou* VII demonstrates the steady progress of China's aerospace industry.

The dream of voyaging into space is as glamorous as it is ambitious. It has captured the hearts and minds of the human race for centuries. China has been pursuing this dream for years, but the country's most recent exploration into the unknown has attracted more world attention than usual. The reason lies in the fact that with the launch of *Shenzhou* VII, China's first-ever spacewalk became a reality.

About seven hours after its liftoff at 9:10 pm on September 25, *Shenzhou* VII moved into the Earth's orbit 343 km out. With one astronaut remaining in the capsule, the other two entered the orbital module to conduct extra-vehicular activities (EVA), and then released a micro-satellite. The three-man crew on board returned to the Earth late on September 28 with a successful landing in northern Inner Mongolia after a 68-hour space flight.

The success of the *Shenzhou* VII space mission will highly improve China's national strength of science and technology, making it the third country after Russia and the United States capable of sending astronauts into outer space. And these historic footprints left by the Chinese astronauts mark a milestone in China's space history.

After sending one astronaut into space in 2003 and completing a two-man mission in 2005, China's latest mission shows the steady progress of China's aerospace industry. Being the most technically sophisticated space project, manned space flight includes seven major systems, namely, astronaut, space science experiment, spacecraft, launching vehicle, launching site, remote monitoring and control, and landing site. This complex process utilizes

the services of more than 100,000 researchers and technicians from 110 institutes and academies, as well as 3,000 units across the country.

During the *Shenzhou* VII mission, astronauts are given a high-intensity workload, including assembling, testing, dressing and undressing EVA spacesuits in orbit. One Chinese astronaut wore the domestically-made "Feitian" (literally means flying in the sky) spacesuit worth more than 30 million yuan, to conduct EVA and recover the experimental devices of solid lubricants, while the other stayed in the orbital module to monitor and assist in case of an emergency, wearing an imported Russian Orlan-M Haiying spacesuit.

In addition, it is the first time a *Shenzhou* spacecraft has been fully loaded with a three-man crew. Behind this historic moment, people often forget the decades of effort made by other Chinese astronauts in the past. In 2005, China established the Astronaut Research and Training Center (ARTC), where the initially selected 14 "taikonauts" (中国宇航员) received intensive physical training and performed countless drills on mission skills and responses to emergency situations. Among the 58 training activities falling into eight categories, each takes the human body to extremes. For instance, in the high gravity endurance training program, astronauts are subjected to a force of gravity eight times their own weight, while trying to keep their minds clear to complete other tasks. The training program can physically burn out these strong men.

It is a symbolic step in aerospace development to manage EVA techniques that are crucial for rendezvous and docking with space laboratories, as well as orbit maneuver and maintenance of the space station. Also, a spacewalk will enable astronauts to perform scientific experiments outside the capsule. The right spacesuit is vital to keeping astronauts alive against the harsh surroundings, zero-gravity, dramatic temperature changes, ultraviolet radiation and scraps of space trash.

The ARTC is planning to groom a new generation of astronauts for future space programs. The astronauts of the next generation will be expected to handle more complex tasks than their predecessors, as ambitious future missions will include launches and dockings of space labs.

Reading Comprehension from PRETCO

Task 1

Directions: *After reading the following passage, you will find 5 questions or unfinished statements. For each question or statement there are 4 choices marked A, B, C and D. You should make the correct choice and mark the corresponding letter with a single line through the center. (2006. 12)*

We don't have beds in the spacecraft, but we do have sleeping bags. During the day, when we are working, we leave the bags tied to the wall, out of the way. At bedtime we untie them and take them wherever we've chosen to sleep.

On most spacecraft flights everyone sleeps at the same time. No one has to stay awake to watch over the spacecraft; the craft's computers call us on the radio.

On the spacecraft, sleep-time doesn't mean nighttime. During each ninety-minute orbit (轨道运行) the sun "rises" and shines through our windows for about fifty minutes, then it "sets" as the spacecraft takes us around the dark side of the Earth. To keep the sun out of our eyes, we wear black sleep masks.

It is surprisingly easy to get comfortable and fall asleep in space. Every astronaut sleeps differently: some sleep upside down, some sideways, and some right side up. When it's time to sleep, I take my bag, my sleep mask and my tape player with earphones and float (飘浮) up to the flight deck (驾驶舱). Then I get into the bag, and float in a sitting position for a while, listening to music and watching the Earth go by under me.

1) When the astronauts are working, sleeping bags are fastened _____.
   A. to the wall   B. to their seats
   C. onto the flight deck   D. anywhere they like

2) Why can all the astronauts sleep at the same time?
   A. They have to follow the same timetable.
   B. The radio will take care of the aircraft for them.
   C. There are enough sleeping bags in the spacecraft.
   D. There is no need for them to watch over the spacecraft.

3) To relax himself before sleep, the writer often _____.
   A. makes a bed   B. gets into his bag
   C. listens to music   D. wears a sleep mask

4) How long does it take the spacecraft to go around the Earth?
   A. Forty minutes.   B. Fifty minutes.
   C. Ninety minutes.   D. Twenty four hours.

5) The best title for this passage is _____.
   A. Traveling in Space   B. Sleeping in the Spacecraft
   C. Equipment Used by Astronauts   D. The Earth Seen from Outer Space

Task 2

Directions: *After reading the following passage, you will find 5 questions or unfinished statements. For each question or statement there are 4 choices marked A, B, C and D. You should make the correct choice and mark the corresponding letter with a single line through the center. (2005. 01)*

The eight airlines of the One-world alliance (联盟) have joined forces to give world travelers a simple way to plan and book a round-the-world journey. It's called the One-world Explorer program.

One-world Explorer is the perfect solution for a once-in-a-lifetime holiday or an extended business trip. It's a great way for you to explore the four corners of the earth in the safe hands of the eight One-world airlines.

You can have hundreds of destinations to choose from because the One-world network covers the globe. And, as you travel around the world, you'll have the support of 260,000 people from all our airlines, who are devoted to the success of your journey, helping you make smooth transfers and offering support all along the way.

The One-world goal is to make global travel easier and more rewarding for every one of our travelers. We try our best to make you feel at home, no matter how far from home your journey may take you.

We can offer travelers benefits on a scale beyond the reach of our individual networks. You'll find more people and more information to guide you at every stage of your trip, making transfers smoother and global travel less of a challenge.

1) One-world in the passage refers to _____.
   A. a travel agency   B. a union of airlines
   C. a series of tourist attractions   D. the title of a flight program

2) The One-world Explorer program is said to be most suitable for those who _____.
   A. have been to the four corners of the earth
   B. travel around the world on business
   C. want to explore the eight airlines
   D. need support all along the way

3) The advantage of the alliance lies in _____.
   A. its detailed travel information   B. its unique booking system
   C. its longest business flights   D. its global service network

4) We can learn from the last paragraph that One-world _____.
   A. offers the lowest prices to its passengers
   B. keeps passengers better informed of its operations
   C. offers better services than any of its member airlines alone
   D. is intended to make round-the-world trips more challenging

5) The purpose of the advertisement is to _____.
   A. promote a special flight program   B. recommend long distance flights
   C. introduce different airlines   D. describe an alliance flights

Reading for Fun

NASA and the Navajo

When NASA was preparing for the Apollo project, it did some astronaut training near a Navajo Indian reservation. One day, a Navajo elder and his son came across the space crew. The old man, who spoke only Navajo, asked a question which his son translated. "What are these guys in the big suits doing?" A member of the crew said they were practicing for their trip to the moon. The old man got very excited and asked if he could send a message to the moon with the astronauts.

Recognizing a promotional opportunity, the NASA folks found a tape recorder. After the old man recorded his message, they asked his son to translate it. He refused. They then took the tape to the reservation, where the rest of the tribe listened and laughed but refused to translate the elder's message to the moon.

Finally, the NASA crew called in an official government translator. He reported that the message said, "Watch out for these guys. They have come to steal your land."

Unit 8
Cloning Genes

Passage A   My Sister, My Clone

I have a clone. She lives in Pittsburgh, Pennsylvania, and her name is Diana. She's my body double: blond hair, hazel eyes and fair skin. She's one centimeter taller, but we have the same voice and the same mannerism. We're both unmarried. We love to read, we relish Mexican food, and we get the same patches of dry skin in winter. We both play tennis and golf. OK, she's funnier than I am—but just a little.

In the debate over the ethical, emotional and practical implications of human cloning, identical twins—distinct beings who share the same DNA—present the closest analogy. Identical twins are in fact more similar to each other than a clone would be to his or her original, since twins gestate simultaneously in the same womb and are raised in the same environment at the same time, usually by the same parents.

But even with the same gene and background, my sister and I are very different people. Diana is a corporate lawyer; I'm a former magazine editor, now a literary agent. She studied classics at Bryn Mawr; I studied the history of religion at Vassar. She favors clothes that have actual colors in them; I opt for black. She's politically conservative; I'm more liberal. She's a pragmatist; I'm an optimist.

Of course, there are ways in which identical twins are bound together that are more profound than the usual sibling links. When I walk into a room it takes no more than a glance before I can sense my twin's mood—if she's happy or tense or upset. I know what it's about and why. It's something I suspect few people, maybe not even all twins, experience. Would clones? I suspect not, since their life experiences would be so different. Other connections between Diana and me may be more related to our matching DNA and thus more applicable to clones. My twin and I filter information in much the same way, and we think, perceive and interpret things similarly. When we're together, we often respond simultaneously with the same word or sentence. We have put on the same T shirt on the same day in different cities. We have friends who are twins, both doctors, who have similar experiences. They took a pharmacy class together in medical school but sat across the classroom from each other and took separate notes. They studied separately for the exam. When it was returned, they had missed the same questions, for the same reasons.

Despite these shared propensities, people who hope they can create a duplicate of, say, a lost child may be setting up that clone for heartbreak. Imagine the expectations that would be created for such a person. Comparisons are tough enough on identical twins. Between Diana and me, there were issues such as who got the better grade, who scored more points in a basketball game, who had more friends. But neither of us had to live with the idea that she was created to match up to the other's best features. A cloned child might not play the piano as well as the original or be as smart.

Identical twins are living proof that identical DNA doesn't mean identical people. My sister and I may have the same handwriting—and a wire that connects us. We have fun with our similarities, but at the end of the day, there's no confusion about who is who. Just as the fingerprints of all individuals, even identical twins, are unique, so are their souls. And you can't clone a soul.

New Words

1. analogy	*n.*	类似，相似	
2. applicable	*a.*	可适用的，能应用的	
3. blond	*a.*	金发的	
4. conservative	*a.*	保守的，守旧的	
5. corporate	*a.*	公司的	
6. debate	*n.*	争论，辩论	
7. distinct	*a.*	有区别的，不同的	
8. ethical	*a.*	（有关）道德的，伦理的	
9. fair	*a.*	（肤色）白皙的	
10. filter	*v.*	过滤，筛选	
11. fingerprint	*n.*	指纹	
12. gestate	*v.*	孕育	
13. hazel	*a.*	淡褐色的	
14. liberal	*a.*	开明的，宽容的	
15. mannerism	*n.*	言谈举止上的特点	
16. opt	*v.*	选择，挑选	
17. optimist	*n.*	乐天派，乐观者	
18. patch	*n.*	一片，一小部分	
19. perceive	*v.*	感觉，察觉，理解	
20. pragmatist	*n.*	实用主义者	
21. profound	*a.*	深刻的，极大的	
22. relish	*v.*	喜欢，爱好	
23. sibling	*a.*	兄弟姊妹的	

24. simultaneously	*ad.*	同时存在或发生地
25. womb	*n.*	子宫

Notes

1. She lives in Pittsburgh, Pennsylvania, and her name is Diana.

   她名叫黛安娜，住在宾夕法尼亚州的匹茨堡。

2. In the debate over the ethical, emotional and practical implications of human cloning, identical twins—distinct beings who share the same DNA—present the closest analogy.

   在由克隆人引发的种种关于伦理、情感和实际问题的讨论中，同卵双生的双胞胎——具有相同DNA的两个不同个体——是最相近的类比。

   DNA: deoxyribonucleic acid，脱氧核糖核酸

3. Diana is a corporate lawyer; I'm a former magazine editor, now a literary agent.

   黛安娜是一家公司的律师；而我过去曾是一家杂志的编辑，现在是作者代理人。

   literary agent: one who acts on behalf of writers，作者代理人

   former: 以前的，从前的，例如，former president，前任总统，former wife，前妻

4. They took a pharmacy class together in medical school but sat across the classroom from each other and took separate notes. They studied separately for the exam. When it was returned, they had missed the same questions, for the same reasons.

   当年就读医学院时，两人曾同时选了一门药剂学课程，上课时分坐在教室的两端，记着各自的笔记，为考试分头进行准备。但等试卷发下来，却发现两人答错的竟是相同的那几道题，连答错的原因都完全相同！

5. Despite these shared propensities, people who hope they can create a duplicate of, say, a lost child may be setting up that clone for heartbreak.

   尽管孪生人有种种相近或相同的习性，但是，如果你希望克隆，比方说，自己已失去的孩子，结果可能只会是心碎。

   propensity: 倾向，爱好，嗜好，例如，The child has a propensity for disrupting class.

   duplicate: 复制品，例如，If you've lost your key I can give you a duplicate.

Exercises

1. Choose the best answer.

1) For what reason does the author say that identical twins are in fact more similar to each other than a clone would be to his or her original?

   A. Identical twins share the same DNA.

B. Identical twins gestate in the same womb.

C. Identical twins are raised by the same parents and live in the same environment.

D. Both B and C.

2) Which of the following is NOT mentioned by the author when she talks about the differences between her and her sister?

A. They work in different fields.

B. They show different attitudes towards life.

C. They have different taste in fashion.

D. Their hobbies are totally different.

3) In the sentence "Despite these shared propensities, people who hope they can create a duplicate of, say, a lost child may be setting up that clone for heartbreak." (Line 1, Para. 5), the word "duplicate" could be replaced by _____.

A. copy   B. parallel   C. repeat   D. match

4) Which of the following statements is NOT TRUE?

A. The author and her sister have the same appearance.

B. Both the author and her sister welcome the comparison between them.

C. Identical DNA doesn't mean identical people.

D. Identical twins are bound together more tightly than the usual siblings.

5) From the last paragraph we can infer that _____.

A. the author and her sister have the same handwriting

B. there exists a wire that connects the author and her sister

C. the author's attitude towards cloning is negative because she thinks every individual is unique and people cannot clone a soul

D. sometimes people cannot tell the author and her sister from one to the other

2. Complete the statements that follow the questions.

1) What do the author and her sister have in common?

They have the same _____.

2) Why are identical twins more similar to each other than a clone would be to his or her original?

Because identical twins gestate simultaneously _____ and are raised _____, usually by _____.

3) What kind of connections between identical twins are more applicable to clones?

The connections which are related to _____.

4) For what purpose does the author cite the example of their friends who are twins?

To prove that the ways in which identical twins are bound together _____.

5) According to the author, what does the comparison between identical twins prove?

It proves that identical DNA _____.

3. Match the following words with the definitions below and then fill in the blanks with their proper forms.

debate	implication	identical	analogy	simultaneously
gene	conservative	corporate	liberal	optimist
suspect	applicable	perceive	duplicate	tough

1) (*verb*) to understand or think of sth. in a particular way

The past is often _____ to be better than the future.

2) (*noun*) formal argument or discussion of a question

The final round of the English speech contest is a _____ on the topic "Meeting challenges".

3) (*adjective*) similar in every detail; exactly alike

This picture is _____ to the one my mother has.

4) (*adverb*) happening or done at the same time

The explosion happened _____ with the plane's take-off.

5) (*noun*) unit in a chromosome (染色体) which controls heredity (遗传)

He believes that shyness is in the _____ .

6) (*adjective*) opposed to great or sudden change

The professor is a radical in politics but a _____ dresser.

7) (*adjective*) tolerant of change; not bound by tradition

He has a _____ attitude to divorce and remarriage.

8) (*noun*) a person disposed to take a favorable view of things

He's such an _____ that he's sure he'll soon find a job.

9) (*verb*) to believe that sth. is true, especially sth. bad

She strongly _____ that her husband had been lying.

10) (*adjective*) capable of being applied; appropriate or suitable

This part of the form is not _____ to foreign students.

11) (*noun*) a copy that corresponds to an original exactly

Please prepare a contract in _____.

12) (*noun*) a comparison between two situations that is intended to show that the two are similar

The teacher drew an _____ between the human heart and a pump.

13) (*noun*) thing that is suggested or implied; thing not openly stated

He smiled, with the _____ that he didn't believe me.

14) (*adjective*) of or belonging to a corporation

_____ executives usually have high salaries.

15) (*adjective*) difficult to do or deal with

Our manager is intelligent and diligent, but is _____ to work with.

Reading Skills

Ⓤnderlining and Highlighting
划线列要点

在做阅读理解题的时候，我们经常遇到的一个难题就是要在有限的时间内读完一篇较长的文章，理解文章大意并解答后面的问题。阅读材料中各种细节错综复杂地交织在一起，有时解题的难度较大，读了后面忘了前面，或者理不出文章的头绪，看不清它的层次和发展脉络，这就对理解全文造成一定的困难。

解决这个问题最有效的方法之一就是对文章中的主要观点、重要信息和细节进行标记和罗列。我们可以用下划线标出文章的主要观点，并用其他符号罗列出文章的要点和重点。这样就可以帮助我们正确地理解上下文的逻辑关系，掌握所读材料的发展脉络，正确解答文章后面设置的有关问题。

划线的方法就是用直线或波浪线标出文章的关键信息。罗列要点就是用数字（经常用数字加圈的方法）把重要的内容一一罗列出来，达到提纲挈领的效果。不同层次的信息点应用不同的符号系统标出。如用直线画出每一段的主题句，再用数字罗列出该段内各个关键的信息点，这样就可以使不同的信息之间不会相互混淆，还能体现出信息的不同层次和梯度。

加下划线和罗列要点的时候，可以直接在原文上划线、标注，也可以在其他地方，如读书笔记、草稿纸上等逐一列出。划线和罗列要点的时候，记号要统一、明显、清楚，使人一目了然。

　　需要划线和列出要点的内容通常包括文章的时间、地点、人物、事件等重要信息点，还包括每段的主题句、关键词、重要的语篇连接词（如转折词、过渡词、递进词等）。用下划线和罗列要点的方法不仅可以节省答题时间，还能帮助我们从总体上把握作者的写作思路和立场观点，而不至于被细节和局部所迷惑，从而提高答题的正确率。

[例] For many of you this will be your last year at school and now is time for you to begin thinking seriously about your future careers. In order to give you as much help as possible, I have drawn up a list of questions that you ought to ask yourself.

"Have I given thought to what I would like to be doing 15 to 20 years from now?" Bear in mind that the career you choose will affect the future course of your life. It will partially determine your range of friends, your choice of husband or wife, where you live, your recreational activities, and other important aspects of your life.

"Have I a clear knowledge of my abilities and aptitudes, as well as my interests and aims?" Be honest about your weak points as well as your strong ones. Take a really good look at yourself and give real thought to the kind of person you are, what you are good at, and what kind of person you want to be.

"Do I know the kind of occupations in which people like myself tend to find success and satisfaction?" Once you have examined and found out about yourself, your next question is what you can really do with yourself. You can gain some ideas of what other people, with similar abilities and interests, consider to be important and challenging in the careers that they chose, by talking to people already in the careers that interest you. Watch these people at work.

"Have I weighed carefully the immediate advantages against the long-term prospects offered by the jobs I am considering?" Will the occupation you select give you satisfaction, not just when you start, but in the years to come? Realize now the importance of education in all fields, technical and professional. Remember that when promotion occurs, preference is usually given to an educated person—other things being equal.

The above questions and their answers should give you some better ideas about how you should start planning your career. Your life-long job cannot be approached in any kind of haphazard fashion. It must be considered carefully, examined from every angle, talked over with those who know you and those who can help you in any way.

  1) The main idea of Paragraph 2 is that when choosing a career we should _____.
    A. choose our career very carefully
    B. make up our mind but be prepared to change it later
    C. choose a career that fits the kind of life we lead
    D. try to foresee how a career will affect our future life

2) The main idea of Paragraph 3 is that when choosing a career we should _____.

    A. decide clearly what we want to do

    B. be honest with ourself

    C. examine and find out about ourself

    D. decide on our weak points as well as our strong ones

3) The main idea of Paragraph 4 is that when choosing a career we should _____.

    A. select the occupation which gives us success and satisfaction

    B. decide what we are best at

    C. compare ourself with successful people

    D. learn from people already in the careers that interest us

4) The fifth paragraph is mainly concerned with _____.

    A. the immediate advantage of the job

    B. education and on-the-job training

    C. long-term prospects of the job

    D. the job salary

5) When we say that a career has "challenges", we mean that it is _____.

    A. demanding   B. easy

    C. well-paid   D. satisfying

在解题前的阅读中，可以先做这样的工作：

1. 用波浪线标出文章中的重要信息——最后一段中的主题句：The above questions and their answers should give you some better ideas about how you should start planning your career. 同时标出重点词questions。

2. 用数字编号标出questions的具体内容，并加下划线标注：

In order to give you as much help as possible, I have drawn up a list of questions that you ought to ask yourself.

(1) "Have I given thought to what I would like to be doing 15 to 20 years from now?"

(2) "Have I a clear knowledge of my abilities and aptitudes, as well as my interests and aims?"

(3) "Do I know the kind of occupations in which people like myself tend to find success and satisfaction?"

(4) "Have I weighed carefully the immediate advantages against the long-term prospects offered by the jobs I am considering?"

用这样的方法，文章的主要框架和写作思路一目了然，解答文章后面设置的五个问题就会更加快捷和容易，而且还能提高解题的正确率。本文的正确答案依次为D，C，D，C，A。

Exercises

1. Read the following passage and list at least four reasons that the author gives to support his view.

I think it is a good idea for women to have a career and a family. There are many reasons. Firstly, if a woman works as well as her husband, the extra money is very useful. Her family can have a better life—more clothes for the children, maybe a new TV and so on.

Secondly, and more importantly, women are not just for looking after children. Women are just as good as men at almost everything, except things requiring strength.

Thirdly, some people say that a woman having a career is bad for family life but, as far as I know, there is no proof of this. In my opinion, it is just a story that men tell each other.

Finally, as far as I am concerned, it is a woman's choice. She has the right to decide. Whether she wants to stay at home or go and find a job, that is her decision.

Topic: It is a good idea for women to have a career and a family.

Reasons:

1) _____

2) _____

3) _____

4) _____

2. Read the passage and complete the following questions.

A new law helps people with disabilities. The law says that disabled people must be able to get into and out of all public buildings. It also says that businesses must offer special services to people who have special needs. Companies cannot refuse to hire disabled workers.

Many businesses may have to change their buildings and services. Ramps (坡道) must be built so that disabled people can get into buildings. Movie theatres must have space for people in wheelchairs and seats for their friends to sit near them. Supermarkets must have wide doors and passages. Lifts need floor numbers in Braille.

This law will help millions of disabled people. One woman has been in a wheelchair for many years said, "It's like a dream."

1) The purpose of the new law: _____

2) Measures to be taken to reach the purpose:

_____ in buildings;

_____ in cinemas;

_____ in supermarkets;

_____ in lifts.

Passage B   Father of the Impossible Children

Read the passage and judge whether the following statements are true (T) or false (F).

1) When Antinori was still a child, he was interested in watching his uncle work on surrounding farms.

2) Antinori began to study medicine before he moved to Rome with his family.

3) Before landing at a public fertility hospital in Rome, Antinori worked in various posts around Italy.

4) In 1986, Antinori resigned from the hospital because he made some serious mistakes in an operation.

5) Antinori succeeded in injecting a single sperm directly into the egg cell.

6) According to Antinori's resume, he had a professorship of human reproduction as well as about 50 journal publications.

7) Top experts, including the creator of Dolly the sheep, supported Antinori's cloning research.

8) Antinori was once president of A PART, an international association of private fertility clinics.

9) The media buzz helped Antinori's daily practice and made him famous among infertile couples.

10) Despite the great cost, Antinori's waiting room is still filled with those infertile couples who are eager to have babies.

Severino Antinori is a physician whose reputation among infertile couples (不孕夫妇) is far over-shadowed by his international fame as the man who wants to clone a human being.

Antinori was born 56 years ago to small landowners in a village of Abruzzi, a region of central-southern Italy. The young Antinori would watch with fascination while his uncle, a veterinarian (兽医), would artificially inseminate (人工授精) cows on surrounding farms. After his family moved to Rome, Antinori signed up for medical studies, where he soon discovered his intolerance for, as he puts it, the "academic mafia (黑手党) that was ruling the university". Still, he met Caterina Versaci there, and the two married shortly after they received their medical degrees. Specializing in gastro-enterology (胃肠病学) and, later, in gynecology (妇科学), Antinori worked in various posts around Italy before landing at Regina Elena, a public fertility hospital (生殖医院) in Rome.

In 1986, he oversaw the birth of the first Italian child to be conceived in a publicly funded clinic through in vitro fertilization (IVF 体外受精). But after clashing with some of his colleagues and hospital administrators, he resigned and, with his wife, set up the Associated Researchers for Human Reproduction (人类繁殖) clinic. Antinori made his mark in the late 1980s, when he pio-neered a technique called subzonal insemination (SUZI 授精技术) to position sperm (精子) below the barrier around the egg, or oocyte (卵母细胞). His work opened the way to intracytoplasmic sperm injection (ICSI精子注射), in which a single sperm is injected directly into the egg cell. He later introduced lasers to facilitate embryonic implantation (胚胎移植). His résumé lists a professor-ship of human reproduction at the University of Rome as well as about 40 journal publications. In the past decade, however, he has become more involved with the judicial system (陷入司法诉讼的纷争中) than the peer-review one.

The world glimpsed Antinori's flamboyance (炫耀，出风头) last August, when he, along with other would-be cloners, including Panayiotis Zavos and Brigitte Boisselier, took on the medical establish-ment at a colloquium (学术讨论会) organized by the National Academy of Sciences in Washing-ton, D. C. Most animal clones die before delivery or suffer from severe birth defects. Top experts, including the creator of Dolly the sheep, Ian Wilmut of the Roslin Institute in Edinburgh, Scotland, revealed that human clones could meet the same fate. Antinori and the other proponents were un-fazed by such warnings. He dismissed the Dolly studies as "veterinary animal work".

Antinori's determination to clone threatens his current livelihood. In September he was expelled from A PART, an international association of private fertility clinics of which he was once vice president. Still, Antinori is not about to abandon reproductive cloning: about 600 infer-tile couples in Italy and more than 6,000 in the US have already signed up for the procedure, he says. And the media buzz has so far helped his daily practice. "He is expensive, but we came here because they say he's the best," explains a patient waiting anxiously while his wife undergoes an IVF procedure. The human imperative to procreate is sure to keep Antinori's waiting room filled—and cloned babies on the agenda.

Reading Comprehension from PRETCO

Task 1

Directions: *After reading the following passage, you will find 5 questions or unfinished statements. For each question or statement there are 4 choices marked A, B, C and D. You should make the correct choice and mark the corresponding letter with a single line through the center. (2004. 01)*

Human cloning technology could be used to reverse heart attacks. Scientists believe that they may be able to treat heart attack victims by cloning their healthy heart cells and injecting them into the areas of the heart that have been damaged, and other problems may be solved if human cloning and its technology are not forbidden.

With cloning, infertile couples could have children. Current treatments for infertility, in terms of percentages (百分比), are not very successful. Couples go through physically and emotionally painful procedures for a small chance of having children. Many couples run out of time and money without successfully having children. Human cloning could make it possible for many more infertile couples to have children than ever before.

We should be able to clone the bone marrow (骨髓) for children and adults suffering from leukaemia (白血病). This is expected to be one of the first benefits to come from cloning technology. We may learn how to switch cells on and off through cloning and thus be able to cure cancer. Cloning technology can be used to test for and perhaps cure gene-related diseases.

The above is just a few examples of what human cloning technology can do for mankind. This new technology promises unprecedented advancement in medicine if people will release their fears and let the benefits begin.

1) Heart attacks can be treated with human cloning technology by _____.
   A. removing the damaged part of the heart
   B. replacing the old heart with a cloned one
   C. repairing the heart with cells cloned from healthy ones
   D. giving the patients injections of various medicines

2) The word "infertile" (Line 1, Para. 2) most probably means "_____".
   A. unable to give birth to a child
   B. with physical and emotional problems
   C. short of time and money
   D. separated from each other for long

3) According to the passage, one of the first expected benefits from cloning technology may be in _____.

A. the treatment of heart attacks

B. the bearing of babies

C. the cure of blood diseases

D. the detection of gene-related diseases

4) Cancer may be cured with the cloning technology by _____.

A. attacking the diseased cells with healthy ones

B. controlling the growth of the cells

C. detecting disordered genes in the cancer cells

D. activating cancer cells by switching them on

5) According to the writer, the main problem with the development of human cloning technology is that _____.

A. it may be out of human control

B. it has brought about few benefits so far

C. people still know little about it

D. people are afraid of such technology

Task 2

Directions: *After reading the following passage, you will find 5 questions or unfinished statements. For each question or statement there are 4 choices marked A, B, C and D. You should make the correct choice and mark the corresponding letter with a single line through the center. (2003. 01)*

Genes that control factors such as size, color and shape determine the differences in fruit. And now that scientists have discovered how to detect different genes, farmers can hand over a young and tender branch to have its genes checked prior to planting. It works the same way as a detective (侦探) checking finger-prints. Once farmers know which trees are good and which are bad, they can discard the bad ones. Farmers can even create new varieties according to their individual tastes.

In the past years, tens of thousands of tests were carried out to determine the genetic (基因的) features of fruit. Zhang, a Chinese scientist, showed a photo of a DNA test and pointed to the shining lines on it, saying that the lines were genetic signs that tell us what a tree's fruit will be like. For example, the ordinary pear tree bears fruit after four years. But now it only takes a month to test the DNA from a young leaf and a farmer will know everything about its fruit. By mixing different types of trees with suitable genes, farmers can create whatever fruit trees they want.

1) Detecting different genes in the plants is like _____.

    A. the examination of human finger-prints

    B. the development of new varieties of fruit

    C. the checking of young and tender branches

    D. the distinction between bad trees and good trees

2) The word "discard" (Line 4, Para.1) most probably means to _____.

    A. put aside   B. give up

    C. deal with   D. take up

3) We learn from the first paragraph that the study of genes _____.

    A. has greatly affected the way of planting trees

    B. has been a popular planting procedure

    C. will change the taste of individuals

    D. will play a vital role in fruit production

4) Now farmers can tell whether a fruit tree is desirable or not by _____.

    A. having a DNA test of a young leaf of the tree

    B. mixing different types of suitable genes

    C. checking its young branches before planting

    D. comparing the shining lines with the genetic signs

5) The passage tells us that the new genetic technology will enable farmers to _____.

    A. increase the DNA of a fruit tree

    B. improve the quality of fruit

    C. make use of the shining features of fruit

    D. change the cycle of fruit production

Reading for Fun

Pet Dog Cloning

A South Korean company says it has taken its first order for the cloning of a pet dog. A woman from the United States wants her dead terrier—called Booger—re-created.

RNL Bio is charging the woman, from California, $150,000 (£76,000) to clone the terrier using tissue extracted from its ear before it died. The work will be carried out by a team from Seoul National University, where the first dog was cloned in 2005.

RNL Bio says this is the first time a dog will have been cloned commercially. "There are many people who want to clone their pet dogs in Western countries even at this high price," company chief executive, Ra Jeong-chan, told the *Korea Times*. The cost of cloning a dog may come down to less than $50,000 as cloning is becoming an industry.

The terrier's owner, Bernann McKunney, gave the company ear tissue, which an American biotech firm preserved before the animal died 18 months ago. She is said to have been particularly attached to the dog, after it saved her life when another dog attacked her and bit her arm.

Unit 9
Defining Success

Passage A   Seeking the Meaning of Life

Drew Gilpin Faust

In the curious custom of this venerable institution, I find myself standing before you expected to impart words of lasting wisdom.

You were asking the questions: What is the meaning of life, President Faust? What were these four years at Harvard for? President Faust, you must have learned something since you graduated from college exactly 40 years ago? Why are so many of us going to Wall Street? Why are we going in such numbers from Harvard to finance, consulting, i-banking? Is it necessary to decide between remunerative work and meaningful work? If it were to be either/or, which would you choose? Is there a way to have both?

You are asking me and yourselves fundamental questions about values. Actually you are worried. I think you are worried because you want your lives not just to be conventionally successful, but to be meaningful.

Finance, Wall Street, "recruiting" have become the symbol of this dilemma, representing a set of issues that is much broader and deeper than just one career path. These are issues that in one way or another will at some point face you all.

I think there is a second reason you are worried—related to but not entirely distinct from the first.

You want to be happy. You have flocked to courses like "Positive Psychology" and "The Science of Happiness" in search of tips. But how do we find happiness? I can offer one encouraging answer: get older. Survey data show older people—that is, my age—report themselves happier than do younger ones. But perhaps you don't want to wait.

As I have listened to you talk about the choices ahead of you, I have heard you articulate your worries about the relationship of success and happiness—perhaps, more accurately, how to define success so that it yields and encompasses real happiness, not just money and prestige. The most remunerative choice, you fear, may not be the most meaningful and the most satisfying.

If you don't try to do what you love, if you don't pursue what you think will be most meaningful, you will regret it. Life is long. There is always time for Plan B. But don't begin with it.

I think of this as my parking space theory of career choice, and I have been sharing it with students for decades. Don't park 20 blocks from your destination because you think you'll never find a space. Go where you want to be and then circle back to where you have to be.

You may love investment banking or finance or consulting. It might be just right for you. Find work you love. It is hard to be happy if you spend more than half your waking hours doing something you don't like.

But what is ultimately most important here is that you are asking the question—not just of me but of yourselves. You are choosing roads and at the same time challenging your own choices. You have a notion of what you want your life to be and you are not sure the road you are taking is going to get you there. This is the best news. Noticing your life, reflecting upon it, considering how you can live it well, wondering how you can do good: These are perhaps the most valuable things that a liberal arts education has equipped you to do. A liberal education demands that you live self-consciously. The surest way to have a meaningful, happy life is to commit yourself to striving for it. Don't settle. Be prepared to change routes. Remember the impossible expectations we have of you, and even as you recognize they are impossible, remember how important they are as a lodestar guiding you towards something that matters to you and to the world. The meaning of your life is for you to make.

I can't wait to see how you all turn out. Do come back, from time to time, and let us know.

Ⓝew Words

1. accurately	*ad.*	准确地，精确地
2. articulate	*v.*	明确地表达
3. commit	*v.*	致力于
4. consulting	*n.*	财务咨询服务
5. conventionally	*ad.*	常规地，传统地
6. data	*n.*	事实，资料，数据
7. define	*v.*	解释，给……下定义
8. dilemma	*n.*	（进退两难的）窘境，困境
9. distinct	*a.*	有区别的，不同的
10. encompass	*v.*	包含，包括
11. finance	*n.*	财政，金融
12. fundamental	*a.*	基本的，根本的

13. impart	*v.*		告知，传授
14. lodestar	*n.*		指示方向的星（尤指北极星）
15. notion	*n.*		观念，见解，看法
16. positive	*a.*		积极的
17. prestige	*n.*		威望，声望
18. psychology	*n.*		心理学
19. recruit	*v.*		招募，招聘
20. remunerative	*a.*		赚钱多的，报酬高的
21. symbol	*n.*		象征，标志
22. tip	*n.*		指点，指导
23. ultimately	*ad.*		最后，最终
24. venerable	*a.*		神圣庄严的；古老的
25. yield	*v.*		产生，带来

Notes

1. Drew Gilpin Faust: 德鲁·吉尔平·福斯特，哈佛大学的第28任校长，也是该校371年历史里任命的第一位女校长。本文是她在哈佛大学2008届毕业典礼上讲话的节选。

2. In the curious custom of this venerable institution, I find myself standing before you expected to impart words of lasting wisdom.
按照这座古老学府别具一格的传统，我站在了你们面前，被期待着给予一些蕴含着恒久智慧的言论。

3. Finance, Wall Street, "recruiting" have become the symbol of this dilemma, representing a set of issues that is much broader and deeper than just one career path.
金融、华尔街、"招聘"已经成了这种窘境的符号，代表着比仅仅选择一条职业道路更广更深的一系列问题。

4. You have flocked to courses like "Positive Psychology" and "The Science of Happiness" in search of tips.
你们蜂拥着去修"积极心理学"和"幸福的科学"这类课程，想从中找到秘诀。
flock to sth.: 一拥而上做某事，例如，People are flocking to the cinema to see the new film.

5. I think of this as my parking space theory of career choice, and I have been sharing it with students for decades.
我把这叫做关于职业选择的"泊车"理论，几十年来我一直在向学生们"兜售"我的这个理论。

think of...as...: 把……看作，当作……，例如，He speaks English so well that he is thought of as a native speaker.

6. These are perhaps the most valuable things that a liberal arts education has equipped you to do.
   这些也许是文科教育可以给你们"装备"的最有价值的东西。
   liberal arts education: 文科教育

ⓔxercises

1. Choose the best answer.

1) From the beginning of the passage, it can be inferred that _____.
   A. it is the usual practice for the president of the university to give a commencement speech
   B. the president has to impart words of wisdom to the graduates because she is old and wise
   C. the convention of delivering a graduation speech makes the old president uncomfortable
   D. the institution's custom aroused the president's curiosity

2) According to the president, the graduates are worrying about _____.
   A. how to make their lives not only successful but also meaningful
   B. the relationship between success and failure
   C. the definition of success and happiness
   D. how to define success

3) What is the implication of the president's "parking space theory of career choice"?
   A. When you choose a career, don't begin with Plan B.
   B. Try to do what you love and pursue what you think will be most meaningful.
   C. It is much easier to park your car 20 blocks from your destination.
   D. Both A and B.

4) According to the passage, which of the following is NOT the most valuable thing that a liberal arts education has equipped one to do?
   A. Noticing your life.
   B. Reflecting on your life.
   C. Wondering how you can gain more money and prestige.
   D. Considering how you can live your life well.

5) In the sentence "The surest way to have a meaningful, happy life is to commit yourself to striving for it." (Line 7, Para.10), the word "striving" means to _____.
   A. stretch
   B. struggle
   C. strike
   D. stumble

2. Complete the statements that follow the questions.

1) For what reason does the president think the students are worried?

Because they want their lives _____, but also to be meaningful and happy.

2) Why do the students flock to courses like "Positive Psychology" and "The Science of Happiness"?

They take the courses _____.

3) To be more accurate, what may be the students' worries about the relationship between success and happiness?

How to _____ so that it yields and encompasses real happiness, not just _____.

4) What is the president's proposal on how to be happy and why?

Find work _____ because it is hard to be happy if you _____.

5) According to the president, how can we have a meaningful and happy life?

_____.

3. Match the following words with the definitions below and then fill in the blanks with their proper forms.

pursue	psychology	notion	commit	distinct
finance	fundamental	consult	conventionally	dilemma
define	ultimately	data	prestige	accurately

1) (*verb*) to go to a person, a book, etc. for information, advice, opinion, etc.

Before going on a diet, it is advisable to _____ your doctor.

2) (*adverb*) basically; finally

As far as I am concerned, the _____ most important thing in life is to do what you love most.

3) (*adjective*) relating to the basic nature or character of sth.

He said that _____ changes had taken place in his life since he became a Christian.

4) (*verb*) to state precisely the meaning of sth.

It is known to all that a dictionary _____ words.

5) (*noun*) idea; opinion

I have no idea of what he means—you know, his head is full of silly _____.

6) (*verb*) to do sth. worthy; to achieve sth. over a period of time

The development of industry must not be _____ at the expense of environmental pollution.

7) (*adjective*) different in kind; separate

It wasn't until yesterday that I came to know that hares and rabbits are two _____ animals.

8) (*verb*) to make someone agree or promise to do sth.; pledge; undertake

The party is _____ to the idea of helping those who are not able to help themselves.

9) (*adverb*) traditionally; according to the convention

_____, the president of the university would deliver a commencement speech this time each year.

10) (*noun*) respect that results from good reputation; distinction that comes from success

At the conference, the general manager warned against any behavior that would mean loss of _____ of the company.

11) (*noun*) factual information, especially information organized for analysis or used to reason or make decisions

Conclusion would not be made unless sufficient _____ are available.

12) (*adverb*) in a careful and exact way

Clocks in railway stations should always _____ show the exact time.

13) (*noun*) a situation that requires a choice between options that are or seem equally unfavorable or mutually exclusive

By making such requirements, you've placed me in something of a _____.

14) (*noun*) the science of the management of money and other assets

He majored in economics and decades later became the Minister of _____.

15) (*noun*) the scientific study of the mind and how it influences behavior

We need some male subjects for a(n) _____ experiment.

Reading Skills

 aking Inferences
推理判断

推理判断是英语阅读理解中常用的技巧。所谓推理判断，就是读者根据上下文内容，从逻辑关系、因果关系、人物事件、行为动机等方面对作者的观点、倾向、态度进行揣测，从而得出一个合理的结论。推理判断不仅能帮助我们更准确地理解文章内容，还能帮助我们进一步欣赏文章。要进行正确的推理判断，一定要从整体上把握语篇内容，在语篇的表面意义与隐含意义、已知信息与未知信息间架起桥梁，透过字里行间去体会作者的"弦外之音"。推理判断题的设置有以下几种常见的形式：

1. It can be inferred/concluded from the passage that…

2. The passage suggests/implies that…

3. The author may probably agree with/support…

4. By the first sentence of the second paragraph, the author means…

5. The author seems to be in favor of/against…

6. The author's purpose of writing this passage is…

7. What conclusion can we draw from the passage?

8. What is the author's attitude towards...?

9. In the author's point of view...?

[例] Why isn't your newspaper reporting any good news? All I read about is murder, bribery, and death. Frankly, I'm sick of all this bad news.

The author's attitude towards the newspaper reporting is to _____.
A. complain   B. apologize   C. amuse   D. inform

此段落只有短短三句话。作者有两个意图：一是说明这份报纸上只登载坏新闻，如凶杀、行贿受贿和死亡等；二是抱怨这样的报纸实在很无趣。 由此推断，作者的态度应是complain。

[例] We walked in so quietly that the nurse at the desk didn't even lift her eyes from the book. Mum pointed at a big chair by the door and I knew she wanted me to sit down. While I watched with mouth open in surprise, mum took off her hat and coat and gave them to me to hold. She walked quietly to the small room by the lift and took out a wet mop (拖把). She pushed the mop past the desk and as the nurse looked up, mum nodded and said, "Very dirty floors." "Yes, I'm glad they've finally decided to clean them," the nurse answered. She looked at mum strangely and said, "But aren't you working late?" Mum just pushed harder, each swipe (拖一下) of the mop taking her farther and farther down the hall. I watched until she was out of sight and the nurse had turned back to writing in the big book. After a long time mum came back. Her eyes were shining. She quickly put the mop back and took my hand. As we turned to go out of the door, mum bowed politely to the nurse and said, "Thank you." Outside, mum told me, "Dagmar is fine. No fever."

"You saw her, mum?" "Of course. I told her about the hospital rules, and she will not expect us until tomorrow. Dad will stop worrying as well. It's a fine hospital. But such floors! A mop is no good. You need a brush."

1) When she took a mop from the small room, what mum really wanted to do was

_____.

    A. to clean the floor   B. to please the nurse

    C. to see a patient   D. to surprise the story-teller

2) After reading the story, what can we infer about the hospital?

    A. It is a children's hospital.

    B. It has strict rules about visiting hours.

    C. The conditions there aren't very good.

    D. The nurses and doctors there don't work hard.

3) Which of the following words best describes mum?

    A. Strange.   B. Warm-hearted.

    C. Clever.   D. Hard-working.

问题1：When she took a mop from the small room, what mum really wanted to do was _____. 选项D与段落信息完全无关，可以首先排除。段落故事背景是在一家医院，而文中两次出现的单词quietly提示读者"妈妈"不想惊动护士，因此排除选项B。段落末尾的对话提示读者"妈妈"见到了某个病人，因此排除选项A，从而推断出该题的正确答案是C。

问题2：After reading the story, what can we infer about the hospital? 由于段落中没有相关的信息支持A选项，因此，可以首先排除；C和D两个选项与段落结尾处"妈妈"说的"It's a fine hospital"有矛盾，因此，也可以排除。联系到"妈妈"是冒充清洁工进入病房的，探视Dagmar时又提起"hospital rules"，我们可以推断出该医院对探视病人的时间有严格规定，所以B选项是正确的。

问题3：Which of the following words best describes mum? 段落主要叙述的是"妈妈"冒充清洁工，在医院规定探视时间之外进入病房探望Dagmar这一事情。掌握了段落大意，我们不难发现只有用 clever 这个词描绘"妈妈"才最合适。

Exercises

Read the following passage and choose the best answers.

CHICAGO (AP) On Jan.1, an order went into effect requiring that every checked bag at more than 400 of the nation's commercial airports be screened for bombs and weapons.

Sunday was expected to be the heaviest travel day since Jan. 1. Yet spot checks on Sunday at several of the nation's airports showed no major delays caused by the new security measures.

At the international terminal for Northwest Airlines at John F. Kennedy International Airport in New York, passengers waited up to 30 minutes longer than usual. Their bags were sent through giant machines and workers tore open taped boxes and searched through their contents before closing them up again.

Most travelers simply accepted stricter screening developed since terrorist attacks on Sept. 11, 2001, before which only 5 percent of the roughly 2 million bags checked each day were screened for bombs.

The US government has put an additional 23,000 people into airports to carry out the new order.

Sonny Salgatar, a 23-year-old college student flying home to San Diego from Chicago, was told by an airport officer after the first pass that one of his bags was "hot", meaning there was something he couldn't identify and he wanted to open the bag for an inspection.

The "hot" item turned out to be Salgatar's clothing iron.

"Listen, anything they want to do for security is OK for me," Salgatar said.

1) The new measure was adopted to guard against _____.
   A. terrorist attacks   B. luggage damage
   C. flight delays   D. air crash

2) The word "hot" (Line 2, Para. 6) most probably means _____.
   A. heated   B. popular   C. expensive   D. suspicious

3) Which of the following is TRUE according to the passage?
   A. Major delays were caused after the security order went into effect.
   B. Most passengers regard the new measure as necessary.
   C. Passengers complain about longer delay at the airport.
   D. There will be more and stricter security measures.

4) What was the attitude of Sonny Salgatar towards the security measures taken?
   A. He was annoyed.   B. He had no objection.
   C. He thought it useless.   D. He didn't worry about it.

5) The best title of the passage might be _____.
   A. Fear of Terrorist Attacks
   B. Latest Screening Technology
   C. New Security Measures Adopted
   D. Inspection of Bombs and Weapons

Passage B   A Commencement Address

Steve Jobs

Read the passage and judge whether the following statements are true (T) or false (F).

1) Jobs quit Reed College once and for all after the first 6 months.

2) Jobs was adopted at birth by a lawyer and his wife.

3) The educational background of Jobs' foster parents did not meet his biological mother's expectation.

4) Jobs' biological mother did not agree to sign the final adoption papers until his foster parents promised that Jobs would receive higher education.

5) It was quite easy for Jobs' foster parents to afford his college tuition.

6) Jobs decisively quitted college because he knew at that time it would become one of the best decisions he ever made.

7) Looking back, Jobs felt that his experience as a drop-in was very romantic.

8) It turned out that what Jobs learned by following his intuition and curiosity was very valuable.

9) What Jobs learned in the calligraphy class did not find an immediate application.

10) Jobs attributed his success in Mac to his dropping out of college.

I am honored to be with you today at your commencement from one of the finest universities in the world. I never graduated from college. Truth be told, this is the closest I've ever gotten to a college graduation. Today I want to tell you my life story about connecting the dots.

I dropped out of Reed College after the first 6 months, but then stayed around as a drop-in for another 18 months or so before I really quit. So why did I drop out?

It started before I was born. My biological mother (亲生母亲) was a young, unwed college graduate student, and she decided to put me up for adoption (收养，领养). She felt very strongly that I should be adopted by college graduates, so everything was all set for me to be adopted at birth by a lawyer and his wife—except that when I popped out they decided at the last minute that they really wanted a girl. So my parents, who were on a waiting list, got a call in the middle of the night asking: "We have an unexpected baby boy; do you want him?" They said: "Of course." My biological mother later found out that my mother had never graduated from college and that my father had never graduated from high school. She refused to sign the final adoption papers. She only relented a few months later when my parents promised that I would someday go to college.

And 17 years later I did go to college. But I naively chose a college that was almost as expensive as Stanford, and all of my working-class parents' savings were being spent on my college tuition. After six months, I couldn't see the value in it. I had no idea what I wanted to do with my life and no idea how college was going to help me figure it out. And here I was spending all of the money my parents had saved their entire life. So I decided to drop out and trust that it would all work out Okay. It was pretty scary at the time, but looking back it was one of the best decisions I ever made. The minute I dropped out I could stop taking the required classes that didn't interest me, and begin dropping in on the ones that looked interesting.

It wasn't all romantic. I didn't have a dorm room, so I slept on the floor in friends' rooms, I returned coke bottles for the 5-cent deposit to buy food with, and I would walk the 7 miles across town every Sunday night to get one good meal a week at the Hare Krishna temple. I loved it. And much of what I stumbled into by following my curiosity and intuition turned out to be priceless later on. Let me give you one example:

Reed College at that time offered perhaps the best calligraphy (书法) instruction in the country. Throughout the campus every poster, every label on every drawer, was beautifully hand-calligraphed. Because I had dropped out and didn't have to take the normal classes, I decided to take a calligraphy class to learn how to do this. I learned about serif and san serif typefaces, about varying the amount of space between different letter combinations, about what makes great typography (印刷术) great. It was beautiful, historical, artistically subtle in a way that science can't capture, and I found it fascinating.

None of this had even a hope of any practical application in my life. But ten years later, when we were designing the first Macintosh computer, it all came back to me. And we designed it all into the Mac. It was the first computer with beautiful typography. If I had never dropped in on that single course in college, the Mac would have never had multiple typefaces or proportionally spaced fonts. If I had never dropped out, I would have never dropped in on this calligraphy class, and personal computers might not have the wonderful typography that they do. Of course it was impossible to connect the dots looking forward when I was in college. But it was very, very clear looking backwards ten years later.

Reading Comprehension from PRETCO

Task 1

Directions: *The following is a general introduction to the preparation of Speaking Notes. After reading it, you are required to complete the outline below it. You should write your answers briefly (in no more than 3 words) in the blanks correspondingly. (2003. 01)*

Before making a speech, we often need to make brief speaking notes. You can put them on cards no smaller than 150×100mm. Write in large and bold letters that you can see at a glance, using a series of brief headings to develop the information in sufficient detail. The amount of information you include in your notes will depend on the complexity (复杂性) of the subject, your familiarity with it, and your previous speaking experience. Here are some steps for you to follow when preparing brief speaking notes.

First, you should write a summary, or an outline, of the project to be reported and the results achieved. Then an introduction follows. This includes background information and purpose of the project. Next comes discussion. In this part, what has been done, how it has been done and the results achieved should be dealt with. At the fourth step, you have two choices: one is the conclusion if the project is completed. The other is the future plan of the project still in progress. At last, a summary should be prepared. In this part, you should give a brief summing-up, plus a question-and-answer period.

Speaking Notes Preparation

Words to be written: in 1) _____ letters

Means of developing information: using a number of 2) _____

Steps of making speaking notes:

- work out an outline

- write 3) _____

- deal with the subject

- draw 4) _____ at the end of the project, or make a 5) _____ if the project is not finished

- give a summary

Task 2

Directions: *The following is the contents of a book on stocks. After reading it, you are required to find the items equivalent to (与……相同) those given in Chinese in the table below. Then you should put the corresponding letters in the brackets numbered 1 through 5. (2004. 01)*

A—acceptance letters
B—adjustment letters
C—application letters
D—collection letters
E—complaint letters
F—credit letters
G—inquiry letters
H—memorandums
J—reference letters
I—order letters
K—sales letters
L—news releases
M—annual reports
N—feasibility reports
O—investigative reports
P—progress reports
Q—trouble reports
R—trip reports

Example: (D) 催款函　　　　　　　　(B) 投诉回复函

1) (	) 投诉函	(	) 咨询信/询价函
2) (	) 推销信	(	) 推荐函
3) (	) 新闻发布	(	) 申请函
4) (	) 进度报告	(	) 年度报告
5) (	) 调查报告	(	) 事故报告

Reading for Fun

Bigger and Better in Texas

There was a very self-sufficient blind man, who did a lot of traveling alone. He was making his first trip to Texas and happened to be seated next to a Texan on the flight.

The Texan spent a lot of time telling him how everything is bigger and better in Texas. By the time the blind man had reached his destination, a large resort hotel, he was very excited about being in Texas.

The long trip had worn him out a little so he decided to stop at the bar for a small soda and a light snack before going up to his room to unpack his clothes.

When the waitress set down his drink, it was in a huge mug. "Wow, I had heard everything in Texas is bigger," he told her.

"That's right," she replied. The blind man ate his snack and finished his drink. After drinking such a large amount, it was only natural his next stop was going to be the restroom. He asked the waitress for directions. She told him to turn left at the register and it would be the second door on the right.

He reached the first door and continued down the hall. A few steps later he stumbled slightly and missed the second door altogether and ended up going through the third door instead. Not realizing he had entered the swimming area he walked forward and immediately fell into the swimming pool.

Remembering everything he had heard about things being bigger in Texas, as soon as he had his head above water he started shouting, "Don't flush (冲刷)! Don't flush!"

Unit 10
Microsoft's Development

Passage A Will Microsoft Still Be Microsoft Without Bill Gates?

Mary Jo Foley

Now that Microsoft chairman Bill Gates officially has begun decoupling himself from the company he founded 31 years ago, it seems like a great time to ask what the Microsoft of the future will look like.

Will Microsoft still be Microsoft without Gates? Sure, Gates is planning to stay on as chairman, though not chief software architect, starting in 2008. Without its competitive, hard-core leader involved in daily decisions, will Microsoft still be the bold and brash company that forced competitors out of business; incurred the wrath of government investigators worldwide; and earned the nickname "The Evil Empire"?

I think Microsoft is going to morph into a very different place, as Gates begins passing the torch to his newly appointed brain trust of Craig Mundie, Chief Research and Strategy Officer, and Ray Ozzie, Chief Software Architect. Ozzie and Mundie, from the limited interactions I've had with them, seem to be a lot kinder and gentler leaders than Gates.

And the world in which Ozzie and Mundie—alongside CEO Steve Ballmer—will lead also is a very different one from the one in which Microsoft has been competing for the past three decades. Commanding a monopoly over desktop operating systems just won't take you as far as it used to. These days, you need to be a leader in search, in online advertising, in software-as-a-service—all areas where Microsoft is a distant third, at best.

I interviewed Gates for the first time in 1984. I was brand-new to covering technology and he was a difficult, fidgety, ornery character to interview. Everyone at Microsoft back then was part of the cult

of Bill. "Bill Reviews" were seen as worse than being sent to the principal's office. He suffered no fools—whether employees or reporters or lawyers. The best Gates insult I personally remember is when the Microsoft honcho chastised one of my reporting colleagues for failing to be "the least bit technical".

Some company watchers say Microsoft already has changed a lot since Gates passed the CEO crown to Ballmer back in 2000. Some believed that move split the company into two factions: The MBA types (Ballmer and his protégés) and the Techno-dweebs (Gates and his gang). During some phases of the company's history, the suits seemed to be gaining in power over the pocket-protector set. But then the pendulum would swing back again, with the nerds gaining freer reign inside Microsoft.

Even though Ozzie and Mundie are both tech guys, they also are both more polished and political than Gates. I would envision an Ozzie review to be more collaborative, kind of like the Groove technology he built and sold to Microsoft last year. And Cult of Craig? I don't see that happening. If the tradition of Think Weeks—Gates' personal time to ruminate on new technologies—continues at Microsoft, I'm betting they'll be more like company picnics than closed, proprietary affairs.

Speaking of proprietary, I'm also wagering that under new management we could see Microsoft start thinking more about open communications, open source, open programming interfaces than it has under the Bill Gates era. I'm not anticipating we'll see the Redmondians open-source Windows any time soon. But now that Gates—as well as long-time Windows chief Jum Allchin, who held fast to a belief that the Web and other Internet technologies were a threat, not an opportunity—are on their way out, I think the 2008+ Microsoft will look and operate a lot differently than it has to date.

It is inevitable that one day Gates would retire. That day is closer than it once seemed. Do you think we're about to see a whole new Microsoft 2.0? Or do you think Gates' succession plan won't mean much for Microsoft, its shareholders, customers and competitors?

New Words

1. architect	*n.*	设计师，建筑师	
2. chastise	*v.*	申斥，责骂	
3. collaborative	*a.*	合作的，配合的	
4. crown	*n.*	王冠，皇冠	
5. cult	*n.*	崇拜	
6. decouple	*v.*	分开，拆开	
7. envision	*v.*	展望，想象	
8. fidgety	*a.*	烦躁的，难以取悦的	
9. gang	*n.*	团体，同伙	
10. honcho	*n.*	老板，大亨	
11. incur	*v.*	招致，招惹	
12. interface	*n.*	界面	
13. nerd	n.	技术迷	
14. ornery	*a.*	坏脾气的	
15. pendulum	*n.*	钟摆	
16. phase	*n.*	阶段	
17. polished	*a.*	彬彬有礼的；文雅的	
18. proprietary	*n.*	所有者，所有权	

19. protégé	*n.*	拥戴者
20. reign	*n.*	统治；支配
21. ruminate	*v.*	沉思
22. split	*v.*	使分裂
23. techo-dweeb	*n.*	精通技术的人
24. wager	*v.*	打赌
25. wrath	*n.*	愤怒，愤慨

Notes

1. Mary Jo Foley: 本文作者Mary Jo Foley 是*Microsoft Watch Newsletter*杂志的编辑。长期以来，一直以报道有关微软的新闻而闻名。当微软总裁比尔·盖茨在2006年6月15日宣布即将在今后两年逐渐淡出微软时，作者即撰写了本文，引起了世人的关注。

2. Without its competitive, hard-core leader involved in daily decisions, will Microsoft still be the bold and brash company that forced competitors out of business; incurred the wrath of government investigators worldwide; and earned the nickname "The Evil Empire"?
没有好胜的核心领导人参与日常决策，微软还会是那个能击败竞争对手，激怒各国政府调查人员并被冠以"邪恶帝国"之名的大胆、自炫的微软吗？
bold and brash: 大胆且自以为是的
incur the wrath of sb.: 激起某人愤怒的，例如，She had incurred the wrath of her father by marrying without his consent.
The Evil Empire: 人们曾把微软比作"邪恶帝国"，因为它在行业内长期独霸市场。

3. I think Microsoft is going to morph into a very different place, as Gates begins passing the torch to his newly appointed brain trust of Craig Mundie and Ray Ozzie.
我认为，当盖茨逐渐交班给他新任命的智囊团——克雷格·蒙迪和雷·奥兹时，微软就将发生很大的变化。
morph into: change into，转变为⋯⋯
pass the torch to sb.: 把火炬传递给某人, 此处喻为"交班给某人"。
brain trust: 智囊团，例如，To aid his election campaign, Roosevelt had gathered together a body of men and women who became known as his Brain Trust, mostly from the universities.
Craig Mundie: 克雷格·蒙迪，微软研发和发展策略总裁
Ray Ozzie: 雷·奥兹，微软首席软件设计师

4. He suffered no fools—whether employees or reporters or lawyers.
他容不得傻瓜——不管是员工，记者还是律师。
suffer no fools/not suffer fools (gladly): dislike being with people that you think are stupid，不愿与笨人为伍

5. The best Gates insult I personally remember is when the Microsoft honcho chastised one of my reporting colleagues for failing to be "the least bit technical".

在我个人记忆中，这位微软老总最具侮辱性的言语是曾骂我的一个记者同事"没有一点技术含量"。

6. During some phases of the company's history, the suits seemed to be gaining in power over the pocket-protector set. But then the pendulum would swing back again, with the nerds gaining freer reign inside Microsoft.

在公司的发展过程中，曾有一段时间那些高级管理人员比核心技术人员更有权力。后来，形势又有逆转，技术精英们在微软内部又重新占据了上风。

the suits: 指代穿着西装的管理人员，尤指因只考虑经济利益而令人不愉快的高级经理。

the pocket-protector: 一种塑料笔袋，放在上衣口袋里插笔用，防止笔漏水弄脏衣服。人们经常把这种塑料笔袋和书呆子的形象联系在一起，例如，Did you see his pocket-protector? What a nerd! nerd指（理工学科的）爱好者，痴迷者，尤指电脑迷，该词通常表示认为这种人很乏味。所以，文中的the pocket-protector set指代的是专门研究技术，精通技术的人。

the pendulum: 钟摆，比喻左右晃动，不断变化的局面，例如，The pendulum has swung back in favor of stricter penalties.

7. But now that Gates—as well as long-time Windows chief Jum Allchin, who held fast to a belief that the Web and other Internet technologies were a threat, not an opportunity—are on their way out, I think the 2008+ Microsoft will look and operate a lot differently than it has to date.

但是既然盖茨以及长期担任Windows首领的吉姆·奥钦——他坚信网络和其他网络技术是一种威胁，而不是一种机遇——正在淡出微软，我认为2008年以后的微软，其面貌和运作都会和现在大不相同。

now that: 既然，例如，Now that you've passed the test you can drive on your own.

be on one's way out: 退出，淡出

2008+ : 2008年以后的

to date: 到目前为止，例如，To date there has been no improvement in his condition.

Ⓔxercises

1. Choose the best answer.

1) From the reading text we can learn that Bill Gates is _____.

   A. bold, competitive and impatient

   B. competitive, ill-tempered and easy to make one nervous

   C. intelligent, gentle but difficult to deal with

   D. brash, forceful and often insults others, especially reporters

2) What is the probable reason for Microsoft's nickname "The Evil Empire"?

A. Its bold and brash character.

B. Its power to force competitors out of business.

C. Its competitive leaders.

D. Its reform and change.

3) How do people feel about "Bill Reviews"?

A. They feel nervous and afraid.

B. They think it a greater honor to see Bill than to see a principal.

C. They are happy and excited to see Bill Gates.

D. They would rather go to see Bill Gates than go to the principal's office.

4) According to the reading text, what will the new Microsoft be like?

A. It will continue to be what it used to be.

B. It will be a little different from the Bill Gates' Microsoft.

C. It will appear quite different from the Bill Gates' Microsoft.

D. It is not mentioned in the reading text.

5) What's the main idea of the reading text?

A. Without Bill Gates, Microsoft will not be Microsoft.

B. Without Bill Gates, Microsoft will be a quite different Microsoft.

C. Without Bill Gates, Microsoft will still be what it has been in the past 30 years.

D. Without Bill Gates, the public will not recognize the new Microsoft.

2. Complete the statements that follow the questions.

1) Why do people wonder about Microsoft's future?

Because Bill Gates has begun to _____ to the new leaders.

2) What does the author think of Bill Gates?

Bill Gates is impatient, _____ and _____ to deal with.

3) What can we learn from the reading text about Microsoft's new leaders?

They are much _____ compared with Gates.

4) Who is in power inside Microsoft?

Sometimes _____, sometimes _____. The situation is not steady.

5) What can be expected of the new Microsoft?

It will be quite different from what _____.

3. Match the following words with the definitions below and then fill in the blanks with their proper forms.

competitor　inevitable　threat　anticipate　colleague

insult　crown　interaction　appoint　succession

architect　competitive　bold　investigator　empire

1) (*adjective*) not afraid of taking risks and making difficult decisions

It's very _____ of the employee to say these sharp words directly to his boss.

2) (*verb*) to expect

Some people _____ that the house prices will fall down, but I don't think so.

3) (*verb*) to choose sb. for a position or a job

Jack was _____ as Chairman of the Council.

4) (*noun*) a person, team, company etc. that is competing with another

By his high spirits and great courage, he finally beat his last _____ and won the gold medal.

5) (*adjective*) certain to happen and impossible to avoid

Don't be disappointed. Failure is _____ on the way to success.

6) (*noun*) someone you work with, used especially by professional people

How to get along well with your boss and _____ is what you have to study further.

7) (*noun*) a situation or activity that could cause harm or danger

This scenic area is closed to tourists because it is still under the _____ of a destructive earthquake.

8) (*noun*) words or actions that hurt or are intended to hurt one's feelings or dignity

Carol will take it as an _____ if you don't come to the party.

9) (*adjective*) able to do as well as or better than others

Our products are of high quality and prices are _____. Moreover, we offer excellent after-sale services

10) (*noun*) a title you get when you win an important sports competition

France will be defending their World Cup _____.

11) (*noun*) a process of acting or having an effect on each other

The _____ between teachers and students are very important in making class activities interesting and vivid.

12) (*noun*) the coming of one thing after another in time or order

We have seven rainy days in _____ and some streets are flooded.

13) (*noun*) someone who designs buildings

He majors in architecture at college because his ambition is to be a(n) _____ after his graduation.

14) (*noun*) a group of countries that are controlled by the ruler or government of one country

The _____ State Building in New York City was ranked number one on the List of America's Favorite Architecture .

15) (*noun*) someone who investigates things, especially crimes

Government _____ are going through the financial records.

Reading Skills

Summarizing
概括总结

　　概括总结就是用简洁的语言复述原文，使读者不必阅读原文全文，只需看一下简短的介绍文字就能了解原文的主旨。进行概括总结时，不要拘泥于原文的格式、时间顺序、语言风格及细节，而要用自己的语言，对原文的主要内容进行提炼加工，去掉枝枝蔓蔓，保留重点要点，不掺杂概括者自身的观点和评论，用中立的语气把原文的主要思想表达出来。概括总结文章或段落，一般来说要注意以下几点：

　　1. 概括一篇文章时，首先要提及文章的标题与作者。

　　2. 通读原文，不仅要注意文章中孤立的事实和思想片段，更要从文章的整体角度来全面阅读，吃透作者的写作意图，对主题思想进行概括。

　　3. 概括一个段落，把段落的主旨言简意赅地表达出来。概括由几个段落组成的文章时，要顾及各段落的中心，把各段的关键信息，用简洁连贯的句子进行表述。有的段落是支撑主题的论证、举例或细节的详述，这些段落可以忽略，删除冗余的材料。

　　4. 概括必须忠实于原文作者的观点和思想。在概括总结时，不应加入概括者对原作的看法与评论。

5. 概括可以与原作的内容顺序有所不同，不一定受原作风格或篇章的局限。

6. 概括的语言要简明扼要，思路要清晰，让读者对原作的主旨一目了然。

[例] My parents imbued in me the concepts of family, faith and patriotism when I was young. Even though we struggled to make ends meet, they stressed to me and my four brothers and sisters how fortunate we were to live in a great country with limitless opportunities.

I got my first real job when I was ten. My dad, Benjamin, injured his back working in a cardboard-box factory and was retrained as a hairstylist. The owner of the shopping center gave dad a discount on his rent for cleaning the parking lot three nights a week, which meant getting up at 3 am. To pick up trash, dad used a little machine that looked like a lawn mower. Mom and I emptied garbage cans and picked up litter by hand. It took two to three hours to clean the lot. I'd sleep in the car on the way home.

I did this for two years, but the lessons I learned have lasted a lifetime. I acquired discipline and a strong work ethic, and learned at an early age the importance of balancing life's interests.

这篇短文主要阐述了作者帮助父母打扫购物中心停车场的经历。这是一份辛苦活，每周三个晚上，持续了两年。虽然不容易，但作者从这一经历中学会了自律和强烈的职业道德。理解了原文，我们可以用下列简明的语言对原文进行概括总结：

Summary: The writer's first job was helping his parents clean the parking lot in a shopping center three nights a week. He did this for two years. It was hard work and had to be done by hand. From this experience he learned discipline and strong work ethic.

[例] I hope you are proud of the accomplishments that have brought you to this important transition in your lives. I know that all of you have worked hard to get here, but let me also acknowledge the contributions of your parents, family members, teachers, mentors and friends who have supported you on your road to Stanford. Without them, the journey here would have been more difficult and less rewarding. In recognition of the tremendous support and encouragement you have received from these important people in your lives, let me invite our new students to show their appreciation with a round of applause.

Students, I urge you to pursue your journey at Stanford with vigor. I hope that this beautiful campus will provide an ideal space for contemplation and inspiration to aid you in that journey. And I hope that you will find an intellectual pursuit that excites you and engages you so much that it will keep you up at night and get you out of bed early, even on the weekend! I hope that you find a passion that matches your own talents, so that you may discover, as I did, something that you can pursue for the rest of your life with enthusiasm and joy.

这是一篇演讲的节选。在演讲中，演讲者提醒学生们要对亲人，朋友，老师等心怀感激，并鼓励他们找到自身的动力源泉来发展他们的才能。

Summary: The lecturer reminded the students of the help they had received from friends, family, and others. And he encouraged them to find their own passionate sources of inspiration to develop their talents.

Exercises

1. Read the following passage and then give a summary of it.

If I thought I'd live to be a hundred, I'd go back to college next fall. I was drafted into the army at the end of my junior year and, after four years in the service, had no inclination to return to finish college. By then, it seemed, I knew everything.

Well, as it turns out, I don't know everything, and I'm ready to spend some time learning. I wouldn't want to pick up where I left off. I'd like to start all over again as a freshman. You see, it isn't just the education that appeals to me. I've visited a dozen colleges in the last two years, and college life looks extraordinarily pleasant.

The young people on campus don't seem to understand they're having one of the best parts of their lives. Here they are with no responsibility to anyone but themselves, a hundred or a thousand ready-made friends, teachers trying to help them, families at home waiting for them to return for Christmas to tell all about their triumphs.

Too many students don't really have much patience with the process of being educated. They think half the teachers are idiots. They just won't know what an idyllic time of life college can be until it's over.

The students are anxious to acquire the knowledge they think they need to make a buck, but they aren't really interested in education for education's sake. That's where they're wrong, and that's why I'd like to go back to college. I know now what a joy knowledge can be, independent of anything you do with it.

Summary:_____

_____

_____.

2. Read the following passage and then give a summary of it.

The following remarks were delivered by the President of Stanford University at the Opening Convocation on September 21, 2001.

Parents and students of the Class of 2005:

Good afternoon and welcome to Stanford University. Today, we celebrate the arrival of 1717 new freshmen and transfer students.

I have struggled with the format of this Convocation and the content of this speech for the past 10 days. Since the morning of Sept.11, the campus has been uncommonly quiet. Except for two memorial services, all major events were canceled. As we considered how to start a new academic year, we decided that a Convocation was, in fact, the most fitting way to resume our normal activities.

Students, you represent our best hope for the future and for peace in our world. Americans and good-hearted people of all ages throughout the world will mourn this tragedy and carry the memory of that terrible day in their hearts. But it is your generation—more so than mine or your parents'— that will face the challenge of building a world in which such inhuman acts can never occur again.

Summary: _____

_____

_____ .

Passage B   ABC Interviews with Bill Gates

Read the passage and judge whether the following statements are true (T) or false (F).

1) Bill Gates decided to contribute all of his fortune to the global health and leave nothing to his children.

2) Bill's mother is keen on doing good things for the community to earn some money for a living.

3) Bill's wife Melinda was often taught by her mother-in-law through letters.

4) In the past half decade, Bill donated $6 billion to help fight against diseases, with a focus on malaria.

5) In Bill's opinion, the resources that have been put into fighting against malaria are not adequate.

6) Bill thought it was the governments that should play a main role in the improvement of global health.

7) It doesn't mean much to Gates whether he'll be remembered by others or not.

8) Gates is always excited at the thought that he can empower people with the Internet and PCs.

9) Gates thinks he is one of the most fortunate, so it is his duty to help the unfortunate.

10) The purpose of this interview by ABC is to reveal Gates' personal feelings and his private life.

George Stephanopoulos, host of "This Week": So how did this all start for you? After you built up Microsoft, made your fortune, you're the world's richest man, how did you decide to start giving it away and how did you choose global health?

Bill Gates: Well, the first thing was the decision that it probably wouldn't be good for my kids, for it to go to them, and so then the question of—

Stephanopoulos: Will they get nothing?

Gates: They'll get something, but not a substantial percentage. Then, the question is how to give it back to society to have the best impact. And so my wife Melinda and I talked about what was the focus in the United States that we think could

have the biggest impact. And then we picked education and scholarships. And then on a global basis, what was the greatest inequity? And as we learned about these health issues, we realized that that's where you can make a huge change and that has such a positive effect on all the other things.

Stephanopoulos: Melinda has said that the night before you got married, your mom wrote her a letter which was a real inspiration. What did she say?

Gates: Well, my mom was very involved in the community, always gave a lot of time in nonprofit activities more than anything else. And she thought that given the success, which was just starting then, that responsibility was commensurate with that, and so very excited that Melinda would be there to partner with me and help us make the right choices.

Stephanopoulos: Let's talk some of the specifics. You've given away about $6 billion over the last five years. And a real special focus on malaria. How did you choose it?

Gates: Well, there are about 20 diseases that don't exist here in the United States that are killing millions of people in poor countries. The worst of those are malaria and AIDS. And so we've made those a particular focus. The exciting thing is that the biology has improved, so the chance of having new medicines and vaccines are stronger today than ever. And yet because the people who need these medicines can't afford them, we haven't put the resources of the world behind us. And with our foundation, with others, with governments now, we're changing that. We're getting the brightest scientists to come and work on these problems.

Stephanopoulos: You said that the way the world is dealing with malaria is a disgrace.

Gates: We should be putting more resources into malaria. The fact that all these kids are dying, over 2,000 a day, that's terrible. If it was happening in rich countries, we'd act. And so making that more visible, getting more resources, I think that needs to be done.

Stephanopoulos: Earlier this year, there was a headline in a Swiss newspaper that said, "The health of the world depends more on Bill Gates than the World Health Organization." Now, that says something about you, and it also says something about the World Health Organization. Flattering to you, but it shows that perhaps we're not all doing enough together.

Gates: Well, the World Health Organization is a critical institution. And we should all adopt the idea of making sure that the best people go to work there and that they get more resources. I think governments overall are the key actors here.

Stephanopoulos: Do you think you'll be remembered more for the work you're doing on global health than for Microsoft?

Gates: Well, I don't care whether I'm remembered. I do think that empowering people with the Internet and PCs is my lifetime's work. That's my job; I'm thrilled about that and the new things we can do there. It's also neat in terms of giving all this money back, to take my position where I've been, maybe, the luckiest person and help the people who have been unlucky to have better lives. I feel very fortunate to have found that and to be able to get engaged and hopefully energize that field as well.

Reading Comprehension from PRETCO

Task 1

Directions: *After reading the following passage, you will find 5 questions or unfinished statements. For each question or statement there are 4 choices marked A, B, C and D. You should make the correct choice and mark the corresponding letter with a single line through the center. (2004. 06)*

Online services are managed by a host system that maintains a base of information available to satellite users. Users of so-called "dumb" terminals (i.e. those without processing capability) simply access the information base via programs stored on the system. Personal computer (PC) users typically access the host through a modem. A PC software program serves as an interface between the server and a PC, allowing the user to operate through the online system and select different databases using a keyboard or a mouse.

National and regional online systems usually have local telephone numbers that PC modems can call to access either a local information base or an indirect long-distance connection, thus reducing long-distance telephone fees. Some online systems allow users to copy large volumes of information onto a local memory storage device, which also reduces the time the user is connected to the online system.

Besides offering a great number of different information bases, ranging from full-text journal libraries to report of missing children, online services allow users to, for example, reserve airline tickets, buy stocks, purchase goods, and communicate with other users. In exchange for the service, users usually pay a monthly membership fee. They may also pay to connect to various databases on the service or to download information.

1) Online services work by providing users with _____.

    A. a base of information   B. dumb terminals

    C. a host system   D. a satellite

2) How can the users of terminals without processing capability acquire the necessary information?

A. They can simply use a keyboard or a mouse.

B. They should use a modem to maintain the host system.

C. They should connect their computers to a satellite system.

D. They can access its base through the programs on the system.

3) If you copy the online information onto your PC device, you will _____.

A. save the time of connecting to the online system

B. reduce the risk of losing information

C. pay just local telephone charges

D. get local information only

4) If you want to read full-text journals online, you usually have to _____.

A. seek for a large amount of information

B. be connected to various databases

C. be introduced by the local library

D. pay a monthly membership fee

5) The passage is mainly about _____.

A. the payment for online services

B. the functions of online services

C. the development of online services

D. the relation between online services and the users

Task 2

Directions: *There is an advertisement below. After reading it, you should give brief answers to the 5 questions that follow. The answers (in no more than 3 words) should be written after the corresponding numbers. (2003. 06)*

Do you sometimes forget birthdays or important appointments? Don't worry! Now you can get help from your computer. There is a new service on the Internet called online calendars. You start by typing in a list of important dates that you want to remember, like the birthdays of your family members and friends. Later, you can add other appointments, plans, and reminders to your list. The online calendar will send you an e-mail message to remind you about your mother's birthday or your friend's graduation day. If you don't have time to go shopping, the online calendar lets you order presents (such as flowers or a book) and pay for them by sending your credit card number. The online calendar also makes a list of your appointments and e-mails it to you every morning. This service is very convenient and easy to use, but it has one big drawback (缺点). You must remember to check your e-mail every day!

1) What is the name of the new service on the Internet?

   _____.

2) How does the service remind you of the important dates?

   By sending me _____.

3) How do you pay for the presents you order through the service?

   By sending the number of my _____.

4) When can you receive a list of your appointment from the service?

   _____.

5) What will you do in order to enjoy the service?

   _____ my e-mail every day.

Reading for Fun

A Smart Italian

An Italian walks into a bank in New York City and asks for the loan officer. He tells the loan officer that he is going to Italy on business for two weeks and needs to borrow $5,000.

The bank officer tells him that the bank will need some form of security for the loan, so the Italian hands over the key to a new Ferrari. The car is parked on the street in front of the bank. The Italian produces the title and everything checks out. The loan officer agrees to accept the car as collateral for the loan.

The bank's president and its officers all enjoy a good laugh at the Italian for using a $250,000 Ferrari as collateral against a $5,000 loan. An employee of the bank then drives the Ferrari into the bank's underground garage and parks it there.

Two weeks later, the Italian returns, repays the $5,000 and the interest, which comes to $15.41. The loan officer says, "Sir, we are very happy to have had your business, and this transaction has worked out very nicely, but we are a little puzzled. While you were away, we checked you out and found that you are a multimillionaire. What puzzles us is, why would you bother to borrow $5,000?" The Italian replies: "Where else in New York City can I park my car for two weeks for only $15.41 and expect it to be there when I return?"

Key to Exercises

Unit 1

Passage A

1. 1) B   2) B   3) C   4) B   5) D

2. 1) promote new products 2) Advertising Standards Authority (ASA)

   3) aped the ad   4) misled customers into thinking   5) not cast for

3. 1) barrier   2) commercials   3) deceptive   4) significantly   5) vomited

   6) epidemic   7) prompted   8) investigating   9) is banned   10) sufficient

   11) visuals   12) acknowledged   13) emerged   14) alerted   15) standard

Reading Skills

1. 1) O   2) O   3) O   4) F   5) F   6) O   7) F   8) O   9) F   10) O

2. 1) Living in a large modern city may not be as good as you think.

   2) a) Wherever you look, it's people, people, people.

      b) The trains which leave or arrive every few minutes are packed.

      c) The streets are so crowded.

      d) It takes ages for a bus to get to you because the traffic on the roads has virtually come to a
         standstill.

Passage B

1) T   2) F   3) F   4) F   5) T   6) T   7) F   8) T   9) T   10) F

Reading Comprehension from PRETCO

1. 1) B   2) C   3) A   4) A   5) B

2. 1) 1,642   2) leisure   3) locations   4) spending limit   5) travel plans

Unit 2

Passage A

1. 1) C   2) A   3) B   4) D   5) B

2. 1) a very serious condition   2) intensive care unit   3) battle to live

    4) calm down and became steady   5) Tears conquered her face

3. 1) bonds   2) complications   3) delivery   4) nagging   5) funeral

    6) conquer   7) miracle   8) intensive   9) steady   10) staff

    11) gazing   12) diagnoses   13) earnestly   14) healing   15) instantly

Reading Skills

1. 1) Dewey   2) Zack   3) Zack's   4) Zack's   5) Zack

    6) Zack   7) Zack   8) Zack's   9) Zack   10) Dewey

    11) Zack's   12) Dewey's   13) Zack   14) Dewey's   15) Dewey

2. 1) people   2) hobbies   3) hobbies   4) people   5) hobbies

    6) cavemen   7) people   8) people   9) leisure time 10) hobbies

    11) people   12) people   13) hobby   14) hobby   15) people

Passage B

1) F 2) T 3) F 4) T 5) T 6) T 7) F 8) F 9) T 10) F

Reading Comprehension from PRETCO

1. 1) C 2) B 3) C 4) A 5) D

2. 1) D 2) A 3) C 4) D 5) A

Unit 3

Passage A

1. 1) C   2) C   3) D   4) D   5) D

2. 1) Franklin D. Roosevelt, the 32nd President of the United States

    2) The Hague

    3) 51 countries

    4) by peaceful means

    5) interfere in the domestic affairs of any country

3. 1) permanent   2) dispute   3) delegates   4) original   5) deliberate

    6) threatened   7) elaborate   8) cease   9) will adopt   10) specializes

    11) Agency   12) domestic   13) representing 14) circumstances 15) interfering

Reading Skills

1) C   2) C

Passage B

1) F   2) F   3) F   4) T   5) F   6) T   7) F   8) T   9) F   10) F

Reading Comprehension from PRETCO

1. 1) G, V   2) T, N   3) O, E   4) K, H   5) D, A
2. 1) G, S   2) U, K   3) Q, F   4) I, R   5) T, C

Unit 4

Passage A

1. 1) B   2) B   3) C   4) D   5) D
2. 1) not easy   2) music
    3) buying all her records and following them
    4) a shy, innocent look   5) one hell of a character
3. 1) alterations   2) veterans   3) innocent   4) cooperative   5) obscurity
    6) engaged   7) costume   8) faded   9) potential   10) aroused
    11) clung   12) collaborate 13) transformed 14) underwent   15) violent

Reading Skills

1) C   2) B   3) C   4) D   5) C

Passage B

1) T   2) F   3) T   4) T   5) F   6) T   7) T   8) T   9) F   10) T

Reading Comprehension from PRETCO

1. 1) D   2) C   3) C   4) B   5) C
2. 1) D   2) B   3) C   4) D   5) A

Unit 5

Passage A

1. 1) A   2) C   3) B   4) C   5) A

2. 1) overcome their own problems   2) a respectable appearance

   3) Mobile phones   4) fiddled with   5) had a great influence

3. 1) addicts   2) fiddled   3) conspicuous   4) altered   5) revealed

   6) casual   7) routine   8) frustrating   9) withdrawal   10) secure

   11) fellow   12) respectable   13) crucial   14) awful   15) diminishing

Reading Skills

1. 1) B   2) C   3) A   4) B   5) C

Passage B

1) F   2) F   3) T   4) F   5) T   6) T   7) T   8) T   9) F   10) T

Reading Comprehension from PRETCO

1. 1) C   2) B   3) D   4) A   5) C

2. 1) the White Pages   2) alphabetic   3) front pages

   4) second   5) separate section

Unit 6

Passage A

1. 1) C   2) D   3) B   4) A   5) A

2. 1) socially, physically and intellectually   2) the perfect frame

   3) organic and environmentally-friendly products   4) to run wild

   5) is the greatest teacher

3. 1) chasing   2) flocks   3) evident   4) intellectual   5) council

   6) abundance   7) context   8) concept   9) stimulation   10) balancing

   11) absorbs   12) contemporaries   13) swing   14) themes   15) variations

Reading Skills

1. 1) Stephen Smith   2) public relations   3) flexibility

   4) broader responsibility   5) (an) interview

Passage B

1) F   2) F   3) T   4) F   5) T   6) T   7) T   8) F   9) F   10) F

Reading Comprehension from PRETCO

1. 1) D   2) A   3) C   4) A   5) B
2. 1) non-native speakers   2) listening   3) language laboratory

   4) video   5) Martin Wilson

Unit 7

Passage A

1. 1) C   2) B   3) A   4) D   5) A
2. 1) clutching   2) before and after they don them

   3) two, free walk and non-free walk   4) deal with

   5) participate and assist in

3. 1) guarantee   2) mission   3) vehicular   4) crew   5) descent

   6) sealed   7) split   8) considerable   9) interval   10) capacity

   11) emergency   12) initiate   13) approach   14) voyage   15) consultant

Reading Skills

1. c-g-d-f-e-a-b
2. 1) D   2) A   3) B   4) A   5) C

Passage B

1) T   2) F   3) F   4) F   5) T   6) T   7) F   8) T   9) F   10) T

Reading Comprehension from PRETCO

1. 1) A   2) D   3) C   4) C   5) B
2. 1) B   2) B   3) D   4) C   5) A

Unit 8

Passage A

1. 1) D   2) D   3) A   4) B   5) C
2. 1) appearance, gene and background

   2) in the same womb, in the same environment, the same parents

   3) their matching DNA

   4) are more profound than the usual sibling links

5) doesn't mean identical people

3. 1) perceived   2) debate   3) identical   4) simultaneously   5) genes

   6) conservative   7) liberal   8) optimist   9) suspected   10) applicable

   11) duplicate   12) analogy   13) implication   14) Corporate   15) tough

Reading Skills

1. 1) If a woman works as well as her husband, the extra money is very useful.

   2) Women are not just for looking after children.

   3) There is no proof that a woman having a career is bad for family life.

   4) Women have the right to decide whether they want to stay at home or go and find a job.

2. 1) to help the disabled people

   2) Build ramps

      Have space for people in wheelchairs

      Have wide doors and passages

      Have floor numbers in Braille

Passage B

1) T 2) F 3) T 4) F 5) F 6) F 7) F 8) F 9) T 10) T

Reading Comprehension from PRETCO

1. 1) C 2) A 3) C 4) B 5) D

2. 1) A 2) B 3) D 4) A 5) B

Unit 9

Passage A

1. 1) A 2) A 3) D 4) C 5) B

2. 1) not just to be conventionally successful

   2) in search of tips on happiness

   3) define success, money and prestige

   4) you love, spend more than half your waking hours doing something you don't like

   5) Commit ourself to striving for it

3. 1) consult   2) ultimately   3) fundamental   4) defines   5) notions

   6) pursued   7) distinct   8) committed   9) Conventionally   10) prestige

   11) data   12) accurately   13) dilemma   14) Finance   15) psychological

Reading Skills

1. 1) A   2) D   3) B   4) B   5) C

Passage B

1) F   2) F   3) T   4) T   5) F   6) F   7) F   8) T   9) T   10) T

Reading Comprehension from PRETCO

1. 1) large and bold   2) brief headings   3) an introduction
   4) a conclusion   5) future plan
2. 1) E, G   2) K, J   3) L, C   4) P, M   5) O, Q

Unit 10

Passage A

1. 1) B   2) B   3) A   4) C   5) B
2. 1) pass the torch   2) ill-tempered, difficult   3) kinder and gentler
   4) the MBA types/the suits, the techno-dweebs/the pocket-protector set 5) it used to be
3. 1) bold   2) anticipate   3) appointed   4) competitor   5) inevitable
   6) colleagues   7) threat   8) insult   9) competitive   10) crown
   11) interactions 12) succession 13) architect   14) Empire   15) investigators

Reading Skills

1. In this passage, the writer praises the idea of education for education's sake and regrets the fact that most college students, motivated only by the idea of future professional success, do not realize what a wonderful opportunity they are missing.

2. In welcoming the new students to campus ten days after the 9·11 tragedy, President of Stanford University encouraged them to help build a world in which such terrible acts can never occur again.

Passage B

1) F   2) F   3) F   4) T   5) T   6) T   7) T   8) T   9) T   10) F

Reading Comprehension from PRETCO

1. 1) A   2) D   3) A   4) D   5) D
2. 1) Online calendars   2) an e-mail message   3) credit card
   4) Every morning   5) Check